THE CASE OF THE BASHFUL BANK ROBBER

The Case of the Bashful Bank Robber

A McGURK MYSTERY

By E. W. HILDICK

ILLUSTRATED BY LISL WEIL

MACMILLAN PUBLISHING CO., INC.
New York

Macmillan Publishing Co., Inc.
866 Third Avenue, New York, N.Y. 10022
Collier Macmillan Canada, Ltd.
Printed in the United States of America

10 9 8 7 6 5 4 3 2 1

LIBRARY OF CONGRESS CATALOGING IN PUBLICATION DATA
Hildick, Edmund Wallace.
The case of the bashful bank robber.
(A McGurk mystery)
SUMMARY: The McGurk Detective Organization joins
forces with the FBI to capture a bank robber.
[1. Mystery and detective stories] I. Weil, Lisl. II. Title.
PZ7.H5463Car   [Fic]   80-24589   ISBN 0-02-743870-8

Contents

1 McGurk Unveils a Surprise

"What are we waiting for, McGurk?"

The speaker was Wanda Grieg. She was standing with Willie Sandowsky and me in McGurk's yard, looking down the four steps that led to the basement. McGurk was standing at the wide-open door, looking up at us.

Wanda was scowling and shivering. McGurk was grinning and—well— not *exactly* shivering. After all, *he* had the heat from the basement warming his back.

No, McGurk was sort of quivering. His green eyes were gleaming, his red hair was glowing, and there was a tense stiffness about the way he stood. Sure signs he was excited about something.

"We're waiting for Brains Bellingham," he said.

"So why can't we wait for him in the basement?" said Wanda.

"Yeah!" said Willie. His long thin nose was turning blue. "It's freezing out here!"

Well, that wasn't quite correct, either. But I could see his point. It was one of those winter days when everything is gray and dull and damp and drafty. Not freezing. Not raining. Not really windy. But making you feel colder and more miserable than if the snow was knee-deep and a gale blowing.

"It's way past ten-thirty," I said.

That was the time McGurk had called his "urgent meeting" for.

"Correct, Joey," he said. He studied the watch he'd been given for Christmas, just a few days earlier. It was a digital watch, almost as big as Brains's watch—the one that told the time in five world capitals, not to mention the phases of the moon and a million other things. "But he shouldn't be much longer."

"Unless he thought you meant ten-thirty Tokyo time," I grumbled.

"He wouldn't make a mistake like that, Officer Rockaway," said McGurk. "Not Officer Bellingham, our science expert."

Wanda gave a steamy snort.

"See here, McGurk! Either you let us in now, right now, or I turn around and go straight back—"

"Come *on*, Officer Bellingham! Move it! You're late!"

McGurk was looking past us. He had gotten even stiffer and was now standing at attention.

I groaned. I suddenly thought I had the answer to all this. McGurk had decided to have a roll call, like the real police! Well, if that *was* his idea—

"Sorry, McGurk! Sorry, fellas!" Little Brains Bellingham interrupted my rebellious thoughts as he came running up. His eyes were sparkling behind his big glasses, and his skin glowed pink through the bristly blond hair on top of his head. Except for McGurk, he was the only warm-looking person around.

"Wait until I tell you *why* I'm late!" he said, digging a hand into his pocket. "Just wait—"

"We *will*," said McGurk, a bit grimly. "Whatever it is will keep until *I'm* through. . . . Right, men. This is the *first* thing I've called you here for at this time."

Without turning around or relaxing his stance, he reached back and closed the door. That's when we first saw the flag draped over the notice. It was held in place by a row of thumbtacks across the top. The

stripes fell straight down, in line with McGurk's arms and legs. The stars were in a cluster just over his left shoulder—like a reflection of the freckles around his glittering eyes.

We stared, wondering what had happened to the old weather-faded notice.

Then McGurk slowly lifted his left hand, put it to his mouth in a cone shape, squeezed his eyes shut—and started making trumpet noises.

And went *on* making them.

On and on. A bit of Taps, a bit of the Reveille, and whole hunks of the thing they play in race-track scenes in the movies, when the horses are entering the track. I mean, the Queen of England couldn't have been given a longer fanfare. Better, sure. Longer, no. And we were just beginning to come out of shock and start protesting, when he ended with a rumbling, coughing, growling noise. (It was meant to be a drum roll, we found out afterward.) Then he reached behind and plucked away the flag.

We gasped.

The notice was a brand-new one. The wording was the same, except for the last two lines. But what impressed us at first was the blaze of color. He must have spent hours on it, using the new paints his mother had bought him.

Here is a copy of the new notice, unfortunately in black and white only:

```
            HEADQUARTERS
              KEEP OUT
      THE McGURK ORGANIZATION
            * * * * *
      PRIVATE INVESTIGATIONS
        MYSTERIES SOLVED
        PERSONS PROTECTED
      MISSING PERSONS FOUND
      MONSTERS EXORCISED
        SPIES UNMASKED
```

Willie broke the silence.

"Hey, McGurk! Wha-what's this about exercising monsters? I don't mind walking someone's dog, but—"

"The word is ex*orc*ised, Willie," said McGurk, smirking proudly. "Meaning 'to get rid of.' Right, Joey?"

I nodded.

"Yeah. Like we did in the Case of the Phantom Frog. But—'Spies *Unmasked*'?"

McGurk shrugged as he began to fold the flag.

"What else do you *do* with spies? What else *did* we do, in the Case of the Snowbound Spy? Uh—in a way?"

"I like the weatherproofing, McGurk," said Brains.

McGurk grinned and stroked the transparent plastic that covered the notice.

"You bet!" he said. "I wasn't about to have the rain wash it out in a couple of days."

"So now that we've all admired the work of art," said Wanda, "do you mind if we come in from out of the cold, McGurk?"

"Not at all," said our leader, shoving open the door. "That was only the *first* of the reasons I called the meeting for. The second is even *more* important."

I guessed it had to be. McGurk was so pleased with his notice that for once he stepped aside and let us enter in front of him. He was obviously reluctant to take his eyes off his masterpiece. He even gave it one last lingering stroke before he closed the door.

So—the way I figured it—whatever else he'd planned for us just had to be of the very greatest, top-priority, Grade-A importance.

2 McGurk's Game

At first, it looked as if McGurk was in the middle of a general cleanup.

The things that were usually on the long table were now on the floor, against the wall. Our files—the boxes labeled #1 MYSTERIES SOLVED, #2 LATEST MYSTERY, RECORDS & CLUES, and #3 DETAILS OF SUS-PECTS—had been dumped there untidily. Next to these, my typewriter had been placed a bit more carefully, with its base resting on the box of typing paper instead of on the dusty floor. He had also taken some care with our new copying machine, resting that on a pile of newspapers.

I decided he'd been using the table itself to sort things on. Right in the middle, there was a shallow

Then suddenly, just as Wanda was reaching out to prod him, he stood up, lifted the folded flag, and shook it loose.

"Right, men!" He bent forward and draped the flag across the top of the drawerful of junk. "The session is about to begin."

He dug in his pocket and took out a bunch of papers: blank sheets torn from one of our stock of notebooks. He slid one to each of us. Then he pulled out four pencils and handed *them* around.

"You had exactly five minutes to notice what is in that drawer," he said. "You will now have another

drawer full of odds and ends of junk. It looked like one of those you get in small bedside tables.

"Take a seat, men," he said, waving to the four chairs, two on each of the long sides of the table.

There again, I ought to have been warned. I mean, the chairs were usually in any old positions. But this time they had been placed just so: side by side, near the middle.

McGurk himself sat in his usual place, in the old rocking chair at the head of the table. His hands rested on the folded flag. He took another careful look at his watch.

"Right, men," he said. "Now for the next important item of business."

He paused, a strange smile on his face.

"Any idea what that might be?" he said.

"If it's helping you to clean out your junk, McGurk, you can forget it!" said Wanda, with a scornful glance at the drawer.

McGurk shook his head slowly. His grin widened. He glanced at his watch again.

"Nothing like that," he said. "Don't worry. This is a genuine training session. Training in a vitally important type of police work. And one we've been neglecting for far too long."

"Like what?" said Brains, frowning.

"Yeah!" said Willie. "What's more important than the shadowing exercises we did already?"

"Or the searching for and grading of clues?" said Wanda, grimly. "Which you keep telling us is top-priority."

McGurk still smiled.

"Top priority, yes," he said. "But *vital* comes higher."

"So?" I said. "What is it? What *have* we neglected?"

He glanced at his watch once again.

"Can't you guess?"

I shrugged.

"Any of you?" said McGurk.

"Uh—the judging of distances and heights?" said Brains, looking interested.

McGurk's eyebrows shot up.

"Hey, that's a good idea! We'll try that one. . . . But not this time."

"I know," said Willie. "You want us to practice holding our breath. Right, McGurk?"

"*How's* that, Willie?"

"Well—you know. Like when you have to dive into a lake after a suspect. Or—or you need to keep close watch on someone without making a sound. Even the sound of breathing. Cops have to do that all the time. They need to practice."

McGurk stared at Willie—speechless if not actually breathless.

"How about judging *time*?" said Wanda, with a glance of apology at Brains. "I mean judging heights is no problem for me, though I admit I *am* a bit shaky on distances. But being able to judge *time*, like in the dark, or without a watch, that really would be useful. . . . *McGurk*?"

McGurk seemed to have stopped listening. At Wanda's first mention of time, his head had dipped to his watch—and he'd kept on staring at it.

five minutes to write down as many objects as you can remember. When I say 'go.' " He was staring at his watch. "A detective's powers of observation must be razor sharp at all times," he murmured. "Now . . . *go!*"

Willie was gaping at him.

Wanda looked like she was going to make a snide comment.

But Brains was already scribbling furiously, and I wasn't far behind.

Wanda sighed.

"Oh, well!" she muttered.

Then she, too, started writing.

"No peeking!" snapped McGurk, slapping Willie's hand as it strayed to the flag.

Wanda had finished long before the five minutes were up. Brains was the next to lay down his pencil—still with a puzzled frown. I kept on going. (Though don't let that fool you. I had a plan.) And Willie kept on going, too. (Though don't let that fool you, either. He'd been at least two minutes late in starting. And he wrote very slowly.)

"Right!" said McGurk, when the five minutes were up. "Put your names at the top and let's see what we've got."

We did as he asked, then passed him our lists.
And here they are:

J. Rockaway

- 1 Typewriter ribbon (used)
- 1 pencil stub
- 1 glasses lens
- 1 eraser (pencil type with brush)
- 1 pine cone
- bottle cap
- old pen knife
- nail file
- ballpoint pen re-fill
- paper clip
- scissors
- ball of wool
- thumbtack
- piece of jigsaw puzzle.

- thimble
- glass marble
- Tube of glue
- screw driver

Wanda G.

\# a pine cone

\# a ladder (toy)

\# a comb (missing teeth)

\# a lipstick

\# a saw blade (small type)

\# a pastry brush

Officer Sillingham

1) Tire pressure-gauge
2) Thermometer (clinical)
3) Compass (directional)
4) Eyeglass lens
5) Typewriter ribbon
6) Nasal spray

Nellie Sardowsky

A Mouth ~~Blo~~ Ball
A Hacsaw Blade
A ~~Hoseal~~ Nose
   Spray
A Bullet

"Well, well, well!" said McGurk, smiling as he leafed through our lists. "Very interesting." He looked up. "Joey," he said, "there are only fourteen objects in that drawer. How come you listed—uh—eighteen?"

I felt my face get red as I grinned back.

"Well, to tell the truth, I only remembered five. So then I figured I'd write down the *sort* of things you find in old junk drawers. Maybe I'll get lucky with a few of those guesses."

"Well, you didn't!" said McGurk. "You got just the five. Out of fourteen. See?"

He uncovered the drawer. We stared at its contents. And I must say this: there'd been no cheating. Nothing was hidden under something else. Every one of the fourteen objects was clearly in view. And when I saw some of them, I could have kicked myself.

Here's the complete and accurate list:

1. Typewriter ribbon (used).
2. Pencil stub.
3. Eyeglass lens.
4. Eraser (pencil type, with brush).
5. Pine cone.
6. Toy ladder (from toy fire-engine).
7. Comb.

8. Lipstick (in gilt tube-holder).
9. Hacksaw blade.
10. Tire pressure-gauge.
11. Thermometer.
12. Pocket compass.
13. Moth ball.
14. Nasal spray.

"Why I say it's interesting is this," said McGurk. "Each of one you noticed the things that interested you most. That's why I chose them."

"How d'you mean, McGurk?"

"Well, for you, Wanda, I put in the pine cone and toy ladder. On account of your interest in trees and climbing. I guess that's why you got the saw blade too, which I really put in for Willie. He's interested in carpentry as well as anything to do with smelling."

"Which is why I also got the nose spray and the moth ball. Right, McGurk?"

"Right, Willie. Though"—McGurk frowned at Willie's paper—"*bullet*?"

"That thing," said Willie.

"Lipstick," said Wanda. "Hey, how about the pastry brush, McGurk?"

"That's a typewriter eraser," I said. "The brush is for the fuzzy bits."

"And I guess the things you planted for me," said Brains, "were the measuring things, the scientific things?"

"Right," said McGurk.

"But I got the eyeglass lens, too," said Brains.

"Because you wear glasses, like me" I said.

"*And* I got the typewriter ribbon," crowed Brains. "One of the writing-material things he put in for *you*, Joey. *And* the nasal spray he—"

"Now just listen to me," I said. "You may have scored top marks with six correct items, but it's only one more than I got."

"And me!" said Wanda.

"And if I'd had time—" Willie began.

But McGurk cut our squabble short by giving the table a slap. "That's enough! None of you've scored anything to be proud of. Six out of fourteen!" he sneered, making Brains blush. "*Five* out of fourteen!" he jeered, glaring at Wanda and me. "And *three*, Willie! *Three!*"

"Well, it wasn't fair!" growled Willie. "There wasn't enough time."

"Five minutes to notice, five more to report?" said McGurk. "Not enough time? Come *on—*"

"Well, you shoulda *warned* us!" said Willie. "They played this at summer camp last year. But they drawer full of odds and ends of junk. It looked like one of those you get in small bedside tables.

"Take a seat, men," he said, waving to the four chairs, two on each of the long sides of the table.

There again, I ought to have been warned. I mean, the chairs were usually in any old positions. But this time they had been placed just so: side by side, near the middle.

McGurk himself sat in his usual place, in the old rocking chair at the head of the table. His hands rested on the folded flag. He took another careful look at his watch.

"Right, men," he said. "Now for the next important item of business."

He paused, a strange smile on his face.

"Any idea what that might be?" he said.

"If it's helping you to clean out your junk, McGurk, you can forget it!" said Wanda, with a scornful glance at the drawer.

McGurk shook his head slowly. His grin widened. He glanced at his watch again.

"Nothing like that," he said. "Don't worry. This is a genuine training session. Training in a vitally important type of police work. And one we've been neglecting for far too long."

"Like what?" said Brains, frowning.

"Yeah!" said Willie. "What's more important than the shadowing exercises we did already?"

"Or the searching for and grading of clues?" said Wanda, grimly. "Which you keep telling us is top-priority."

McGurk still smiled.

"Top priority, yes," he said. "But *vital* comes higher."

"So?" I said. "What is it? What *have* we neglected?"

He glanced at his watch once again.

"Can't you guess?"

I shrugged.

"Any of you?" said McGurk.

"Uh—the judging of distances and heights?" said Brains, looking interested.

McGurk's eyebrows shot up.

"Hey, that's a good idea! We'll try that one. . . . But not this time."

"I know," said Willie. "You want us to practice holding our breath. Right, McGurk?"

"*How's* that, Willie?"

"Well—you know. Like when you have to dive in-to a lake after a suspect. Or—or you need to keep close watch on someone without making a sound. Even the sound of breathing. Cops have to do that all the time. They need to practice."

McGurk stared at Willie—speechless if not actually breathless.

"How about judging *time*?" said Wanda, with a glance of apology at Brains. "I mean judging heights is no problem for me, though I admit I *am* a bit shaky on distances. But being able to judge *time*, like in the dark, or without a watch, that really would be useful. . . . *McGurk*?"

McGurk seemed to have stopped listening. At Wanda's first mention of time, his head had dipped to his watch—and he'd kept on staring at it.

Then suddenly, just as Wanda was reaching out to prod him, he stood up, lifted the folded flag, and shook it loose.

"Right, men!" He bent forward and draped the flag across the top of the drawerful of junk. "The session is about to begin."

He dug in his pocket and took out a bunch of papers: blank sheets torn from one of our stock of notebooks. He slid one to each of us. Then he pulled out four pencils and handed *them* around.

"You had exactly five minutes to notice what is in that drawer," he said. "You will now have another

five minutes to write down as many objects as you
can remember. When I say 'go.'" He was staring at
his watch. "A detective's powers of observation must
be razor sharp at all times," he murmured. "Now
. . . *go!*"

Willie was gaping at him.

Wanda looked like she was going to make a snide
comment.

But Brains was already scribbling furiously, and
I wasn't far behind.

Wanda sighed.

"Oh, well!" she muttered.

Then she, too, started writing.

"No peeking!" snapped McGurk, slapping Willie's
hand as it strayed to the flag.

Wanda had finished long before the five minutes
were up. Brains was the next to lay down his pencil—still with a puzzled frown. I kept on going.
(Though don't let that fool you. I had a plan.) And
Willie kept on going, too. (Though don't let that fool
you, either. He'd been at least two minutes late in
starting. And he wrote very slowly.)

"Right!" said McGurk, when the five minutes
were up. "Put your names at the top and let's see
what we've got."

We did as he asked, then passed him our lists.
And here they are:

J. Rockaway

- 1 Typewriter ribbon (used)
- 1 pencil stub
- 1 glasses lens
- 1 eraser (pencil type with brush)
- 1 pine cone
- bottle cap
- old pen knife
- nail file
- ballpoint pen refill
- paper clip
- scissors
- ball of wool
- thumbtack
- piece of jigsaw puzzle.
- thimble
- glass marble
- Tube of glue
- screw driver

Wanda G.

- # a pine cone
- # a ladder (toy)
- # a comb (missing teeth)
- # a lipstick
- # a saw blade (small type)
- # a pastry brush

Officer Bellingham
1) Tire pressure-gauge
2) Thermometer (clinical)
3) Compass (directional)
4) Eyeglass lens
5) Typewriter ribbon
6) Nasal spray

Nellie Sandowsky
A Mouth ~~Blo~~ Ball
A Hacsaw Blade
A ~~Noreat~~ Nose
Spray
A Bullet

"Well, well, well!" said McGurk, smiling as he leafed through our lists. "Very interesting." He looked up. "Joey," he said, "there are only fourteen objects in that drawer. How come you listed—uh—eighteen?"

I felt my face get red as I grinned back.

"Well, to tell the truth, I only remembered five. So then I figured I'd write down the *sort* of things you find in old junk drawers. Maybe I'll get lucky with a few of those guesses."

"Well, you didn't!" said McGurk. "You got just the five. Out of fourteen. See?"

He uncovered the drawer. We stared at its contents. And I must say this: there'd been no cheating. Nothing was hidden under something else. Every one of the fourteen objects was clearly in view. And when I saw some of them, I could have kicked myself.

Here's the complete and accurate list:

1. Typewriter ribbon (used).
2. Pencil stub.
3. Eyeglass lens.
4. Eraser (pencil type, with brush).
5. Pine cone.
6. Toy ladder (from toy fire-engine).
7. Comb.

8. Lipstick (in gilt tube-holder).
9. Hacksaw blade.
10. Tire pressure-gauge.
11. Thermometer.
12. Pocket compass.
13. Moth ball.
14. Nasal spray.

"Why I say it's interesting is this," said McGurk. "Each of one you noticed the things that interested you most. That's why I chose them."

"How d'you mean, McGurk?"

"Well, for you, Wanda, I put in the pine cone and toy ladder. On account of your interest in trees and climbing. I guess that's why you got the saw blade too, which I really put in for Willie. He's interested in carpentry as well as anything to do with smell-ing."

"Which is why I also got the nose spray and the moth ball. Right, McGurk?"

"Right, Willie. Though"—McGurk frowned at Willie's paper—"*bullet*?"

"That thing," said Willie.

"Lipstick," said Wanda. "Hey, how about the pastry brush, McGurk?"

"That's a typewriter eraser," I said. "The brush is for the fuzzy bits."

"And I guess the things you planted for me," said Brains, "were the measuring things, the scientific things?"

"Right," said McGurk.

"But I got the eyeglass lens, too," said Brains.

"Because you wear glasses, like me" I said.

"*And* I got the typewriter ribbon," crowed Brains. "One of the writing-material things he put in for *you*, Joey. *And* the nasal spray he—"

"Now just listen to me," I said. "You may have scored top marks with six correct items, but it's only one more than I got."

"And me!" said Wanda.

"And if I'd had time—" Willie began.

But McGurk cut our squabble short by giving the table a slap. "That's enough! None of you've scored anything to be proud of. Six out of fourteen!" he sneered, making Brains blush. "*Five* out of fourteen!" he jeered, glaring at Wanda and me. "And *three*, Willie! *Three!*"

"Well, it wasn't fair!" growled Willie. "There wasn't enough time."

"Five minutes to notice, five more to report?" said McGurk. "Not enough time? Come *on*—"

"Well, you shoulda *warned* us!" said Willie. "They played this at summer camp last year. But they warned us first and then gave us exactly sixty seconds to look before they covered the things up."

"That's right," I said. "Sixty seconds with a warning is a whole lot better than five minutes without any warning. It's called Kim's Game, by the way. From a book called—"

Again McGurk slapped the table.

"And this is called *McGurk's* Game! Only it isn't a game. It's a vital training exercise. For detectives. Who must be observant at all times."

"But—"

But there was no stopping McGurk now.

"Do you think bank robbers holler out, *'This is a stickup. You have sixty seconds to look at us and remember how tall we are and what we're wearing, and like that. Then you all go face down on the floor and close your eyes or get your heads blown off.'?* Huh? No way! So—"

"Hey! McGurk! That reminds me!"

"Do not interrupt, Officer Bellingham!"

But Brains was already pulling some news clippings from his pocket.

"Bank robbers," he said. "It looks like they're headed this way. The papers say the police and FBI should put out a Red Alert over the whole area."

"Let me *see* those!" said McGurk, reaching out.

Judging from the gleam in his eyes, all thoughts of his "vitally important" training session had flown clear from his head.

3 Red Alert

McGurk wasn't the only one to drop all ideas about training sessions.

Don't forget, this was just after Christmas. Gifts had started to fall apart. The cold turkey kept staggering onto the table for meal after meal. Parents were beginning to get grouchy. The weather had also failed us. Snow had come early this year, but by Christmas—just when we kids needed it—it had cleared away.

So we were bored. Even school would have been a relief, but that didn't open for another ten days. Even McGurk's training sessions would have broken the monotony. Why else did we rush to answer his call?

But this talk about bank robbers was something else. The possibility of another case—and such a juicy one—set us all tingling. We stared at the clippings.

The banner headlines actually started my mouth watering. Here they are:

Bank-Heist Wave Heading This Way

N.Y.C. TASK FORCE SUCCESS "TWO-EDGED"

"COULD BE BAD NEWS FOR NEARBY TOWNS"

Latest crime figures released today by the

"Hey, read it out loud, McGurk!" said Willie. "I can't read the small print from here."

"Sure!" McGurk cleared his throat. "*Latest crime figures released today by the New York City Police Department show a dramatic drop in the number of bank robberies in the city area. The—*"

"So why all this about a Red Alert?" said Wanda.

"He'll be getting to that," said Brains. "This was clipped from last night's *Gazette and Advertiser*, the local paper. It goes on to tell you the effect that—"

"Do you want me to read this out or not?" growled McGurk.

Brains closed his mouth. Wanda dipped her head.

"O.K.," said McGurk. "It goes on: *The police spokesman said yesterday that this was largely due to the special NYPD/FBI Task Force—*"

"Wow!" said Willie. "The FBI!"

We knew how he felt. The initials had sent a thrill through the rest of us, too.

"*—which has been fighting bank robbers in the city for the past six months. . . . Hard Core. . . .*" McGurk looked up. "That's this little heading here, over the next bit."

"Go *on*, McGurk!" said Wanda.

McGurk continued.

"*Especially heartening is the fact that armed robberies by gangs of two or more have decreased by fifty percent. These are mainly the hard-core professionals. They are obviously being scared off, at least for the time being.*

"I would be, too!" said Willie. "If the police *and* the FBI were on my tail!"

McGurk nodded.

"Right, Willie. And if the police plus the FBI plus *The McGurk Organization* were out to get you, you'd be even scareder. Right?"

"Go on, McGurk," I said. "What's this next bit? Something about—uh—*note jobs*. . . ."

"Yeah." McGurk cleared his throat again. "It says: *It is significant that most of the bank robberies taking place in the last few weeks have been note jobs —casual, off-the-street, amateur attempts.*"

"What are note jobs?"

"If you listen, maybe it'll *tell* you!" said McGurk, frowning at the clipping. He read on, more slowly: "*Asked what he meant by 'note jobs,' the spokesman explained: 'These are attempted by perpetrators who walk in off the street, line up with the regular customers, and slip the teller a note. The notes usually say,* "I have a gun—or a bomb—and I will use it if you don't fill up this brown bag with tens, twenties and fifties." *These people are usually bluffing. They rarely carry any weapons. They rarely score more than a few hundred dollars. And most are apprehended within a couple of blocks of the bank.'*"

"*Penny ante!*" said Willie scornfully, like he'd been working on a top NYPD/FBI Task Force all his life.

"Sure!" said McGurk, like *he'd* been *in charge of* that same Task Force all his life. "But here's what it says about the real pro bank robbers. . . . *When*

asked if there was a danger of the professional armed robbers turning their attention to smaller cities and townships near New York, the police spokesman said: 'I am only concerned with the figures for the NYPD area.' The FBI spokesman was even cagier. 'No comment' was his only answer."

"Right!" said Brains. "But now read out the next bit, McGurk. This is the part that made my hair bristle."

"Mine too!" murmured McGurk, his eyes widening.

"Come on, McGurk!" said Wanda.

"Listen to *this!*" said McGurk. "Just *listen!* . . . *Mr. Sam Marshall, President of the County Chamber of Commerce, was more outspoken. Addressing members of the Rotary Club at their annual general meeting and dinner last night, he said: 'The signs are already loud and clear. Hard-core armed robberies of banks are already on the upturn in the suburbs. No time should be lost in forming task forces of local police agencies and the FBI, similar to the one in New York City. The whole suburban area should be put on Red Alert.'*"

"See what I mean?" said Brains, his eyes shining.

"The robbers are coming!" cried Willie, sounding like Paul Revere.

"It certainly *looks* that way!" said Wanda, flicking her hair from side to side in her excitement.

"*Red Alert,*" murmured McGurk. "I like it, I like it. . . ." He looked up. "Men," he said, thumping the table, "that is exactly what the Organization is on, as of right now. Red Bank-Robber Alert. Let's start making plans."

4 Getaway Car?

Making plans didn't take long.

"First, we draw up a list of all the banks down-town," said McGurk. "With exact locations."

"But I never notice banks!" said Willie. "I've never even been in one!"

"So what?" said McGurk. "All we have to do is look in the Yellow Pages. Under 'Banks.' And pick them out of there."

And we did. There were seven. When we were quite sure we hadn't overlooked any, McGurk took a sheet of my typing paper and started drawing a map.

"Luckily they're all in one fairly small area," he said. He glanced at the list. "Three of them along Main Street." He marked the locations with X's.

"Then there's this one on Elm. . . . One on Taft Avenue. . . . Another on Willow. . . . And—oh, yeah —this one on the Station Plaza."

"Aren't you going to write in their names?" asked Wanda.

"Not enough space," grunted McGurk. (He was right. Most of them had long rambling titles like *The Federal Savings and Mutual Trust Bank of New York*.) "We'll just call them A, B, C, and like that. In regular order. So it'll be easy to patrol them."

"*Patrol* them?" said Brains.

But McGurk was too busy to reply—slowly, deliberately, adding the letters.

"There!" he said, when each of the seven banks had been marked in this way.

We studied the result. Here is a copy:

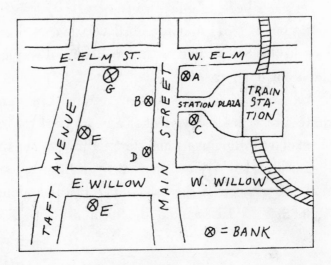

"See what I mean about regular patrolling?"

"Sure," said Wanda. "We start at A, move onto B, take in C, go across to D, then around through E and F to G."

"Correct! Then back across to A and follow the same route all over."

"Clockwise," said Brains. "Neat idea, McGurk. Nice and systematic."

"Any questions?" said McGurk.

"Yes. What exactly will we be looking for?" asked Wanda. "Suspicious-looking characters?"

McGurk's face shone as he shook his head.

"Something a whole lot more obvious than that, Officer Grieg. What we'll be looking for, at each of these locations, will be any signs of a getaway car."

"A—a getaway car?"

"Sure, Willie. We're looking for real hard-core professional armed bank robbers. And they *always* use getaway cars—all ready with motors running outside the bank."

I could see his point. We all could. None of us raised a word of protest after that. No one bothered with any further questions. We were all too eager to get out and away downtown and start our patrol. Well, almost right away we seemed to get lucky.

"Hey!" gasped Willie, pointing across Main Street toward Bank D. "Is *that* one?"

We'd just emerged from Station Plaza, having checked Banks A, B and C.

"Act *casual!*" hissed McGurk, slapping down Willie's pointing finger.

But his face had turned bright red. I felt my own cheeks coloring. Wanda's breath started coming faster and raspier, and the sudden nervous flick she gave the right wing of her hair might have knocked Brains's glasses clean off his nose, if he hadn't already taken them off to give them a quick polishing. (*His* sign of nerves.)

For there, parked right outside the bank, was a speedy-looking late-model black Mercury. Gusts of steamy smoke from the exhaust were bursting in the raw damp air, as the driver kept revving his engine.

As for the driver himself, if ever I saw a hardened criminal, this was one. He had a long pale face with a hawklike nose and lips set in a thin straight line. His hat brim came well down over his eyes, making it hard to see them—but I'd no doubt they were small and mean and slitty, and constantly flitting from side to side.

"What—what now, McGurk?" asked Wanda.

"Take its number, Joey, take its number!" said Brains, almost dancing with excitement.

"No!" said McGurk, putting a hand on my arm. "It'll only waste time. The car's bound to be stolen anyway. They'll only dump it and get another."

"Should we phone the cops?" said Willie.

"Not enough time," said McGurk. "Any second now, the rest of the gang could come out. Shooting . . . . No, men. We immobilize the car. We go across there and quickly but very quietly—so he doesn't suspect a thing—we let the air out of his back tires . . . . Come on. Keep it casual."

He started crossing the street toward the rear of the car.

"You mean—*puncture* them?" asked Wanda. "But —but suppose he's innocent?"

"Hah! Fat chance of *that!*" said McGurk. We had now reached the opposite sidewalk. "But anyway, I was thinking of something quieter. Just letting the air out the *normal* way. . . . Uh—Brains. You were the only one to recognize the tire pressure-gauge back at HQ. Think you can handle this?"

"Well—sure—I suppose so."

"O.K., then. Get busy on the rear curbside wheel. Joey, you cover him. Pretend to be pulling a pebble out of your shoe or something. You others, come with me. We'll pretend to be looking in this store window next to the bank. If Brains and Joey fail, we'll just have to fling ourselves at the feet of the robbers when they come running out."

I hadn't time to study Wanda's and Willie's faces on receiving *that* instruction. Brains was already stooping at the side of the rear wheel. I loosened my coat to form a better screen and crouched to join him.

Well, one thing I have to report right now is that letting air out of a car tire is no cinch. A bicycle tire—O.K. You just turn a screw and there you go. But a car tire needs more than just fingers.

Brains tried. And Brains failed.

"We need a special tool, a special tool!" he gasped.

He was getting more than just nervous. He was getting mad too—all his scientific pride hurt. Still crouching, he was doing a kind of hopping on the spot, like a little angry frog.

I saw what he meant. Finding the nozzle had been no problem. But the valve itself—the little shiny part that had to be pushed farther in to release the air—this valve nestled inside the nozzle out of reach of even Brains's bony little fingers.

"Your knife," I said. "Your Swiss Army knife. Got it?"

All the time, people were passing. I was beginning to feel the strain in my knees.

"Sure!" said Brains. "But I can't *slash* the tire. You—oh, I see what you mean!"

His cool scientific brain must have taken over again. Rapidly, he plucked at the knife, releasing and rejecting a small blade, a corkscrew and a can opener, before settling for the short blunt spike that he'd once told me was for prying stones out of horses' hooves.

And he was just about to push the spike into the nozzle, to press down the valve, when we heard the woman yell.

"What's going *on* here?"

We looked up. She was standing over us. A short dumpy woman, with very thick muscular legs and a very fierce expression.

I caught a glimpse of McGurk and the others, behind her. They were shrinking against the store window. Their eyes were wide with horror and confusion.

"We—were . . . ."

Brains trailed off. She was glaring at the knife and I guess it had suddenly occurred to Brains how bad things looked.

"He—he was just trying to— to get a piece of—of stone—out of my shoe," I whispered. She gave an angry growl. Then she reached over, banged on the car roof, and yelled: "Justin! You'd better get out and see about this! Right now!"

5 Machine-Gun Kelly

I have to correct one thing.

When the driver stepped out of the car, I saw that his eyes were *not* slitty and shifty. They were quite big and very steady. Hard, yes. Gray as steel, and hard as steel.

They seemed to get even grayer and harder as they stared at the Swiss Army knife in Brains's hand.

"These vandals were just about to slash the tires, Justin!"

"They were *what*?" he growled.

His voice rasped like a file biting into more steel.

"No, sir! No, ma'am! You've got it all wrong!" This was McGurk.

And let me say it again about McGurk. For all his faults, he never, ever deserts his friends. When any of his dumb, crazy schemes goes wrong, he's always ready to take his share of blame.

"Responsibility," he calls it.

He called it that now.

"I take full responsibility for my officers' actions."

" 'Officers?!' " said the man and woman together making a rasp and a screech.

"ID cards, men!" said McGurk.

We took out our ID cards—Wanda and Willie included. Quite a crowd had started to gather.

The man's eyes ignored the cards. They stayed fixed on McGurk's face.

"Explain yourself!"

Something about that command and the way he said it made my heart sink. I knew I'd been wrong about his eyes, but if this wasn't a *teacher*, my name wasn't Joey Rockaway.

"You see, sir," McGurk was explaining, "we're on Red Alert—Red Bank-Robber Alert. And seeing your car parked here, right outside the bank, with the engine running, we felt sure you were—uh—a wheelsman."

"A *wheelsman*?!" yelped the woman.

"Yes, ma'am. You know. The driver of a getaway car."

The man growled wordlessly. The woman yelped again.

"My *husband*? The driver of a *getaway* car?"

"Leave this to me, Mildred." The driver turned to McGurk. "For your information, young man, I happen to be a teacher." (*"There!"* I thought. *"I knew it!"*) "I happen to be a teacher with wide experience of students like you. And *I* feel certain that you and your friends are the sort of fresh, undisciplined, mischievous young idiots who think it smart to mock authority!"

"Authority, sir?"

"Yes. Don't try to tell me you don't know who I

am. No doubt you saw my picture in last Saturday's paper."

We stared at each other. Some of us shrugged. None of us had any idea what he was talking about.

"But—"

"So you thought you could earn a reputation by slashing my tires."

"*Slashing?*" cried Brains. "No! No, sir! I was only going to let the air out!"

"Hah!" yelped the woman. "So now they admit it!"

"*Problem, folks?*"

We all turned. The newcomer was Patrolman Cassidy. McGurk looked relieved. Patrolman Cassidy is a good friend of ours. Why, he'd even donated the old pair of handcuffs that hangs on the wall of our HQ!

"*He'll* tell you!" McGurk said. "Mr. Cassidy! Please tell them we're not vandals. Tell them we're a *detective* organization."

"Sure, sure. . . ." The elderly cop patted McGurk's shoulder as he gazed steadily at the man. "I don't know exactly what they're supposed to have done, sir, but—"

"Letting the air out of our tires!" said the woman. "That's what."

"We only *intended* to," said McGurk. "And that's

only because we thought he was the wheelsman for a bank holdup. You *know*, Mr. Cassidy. Like with all the bank robbers ready to switch from New York and head this way. Like—like in the paper, last night."

"Ah, yes." The cop stroked his chin. He winked at the man and woman. "I did hear some talk of that. . . ." But the man and woman didn't wink back. They just glared. So a hard glint came into Mr. Cassidy's eyes. "And with the car being parked right here," he said slowly, turning to McGurk, "you naturally—"

"Officer!" the man butted in. "I'll have you know that I've had wide experience with young people and—"

"Is that so, sir?" said Patrolman Cassidy, who'd been looking even more annoyed since the interruption. "Well so have I. I happen to be schools liaison officer for this city, and you can take it from me—"

Again the man didn't let him finish.

"Really? Well, we shall soon be getting to know each other better, in that case. My name is Kelly. Justin Kelly. I shall be taking over as principal of the Junior High School here when Mr. Michaels retires at Easter."

"Yes," said the woman. "In fact we're here on a

preliminary visit. I was just inquiring about opening a new bank account. Then I find *this* happening. Wheelsman indeed!"

Mr. Kelly's announcement had shocked us. Even McGurk was speechless. The new principal seemed to read our minds.

"I should judge you all to be still in elementary school. Eleven years old or thereabouts. Maybe ten." he added, giving Brains a hard stare that caused our science expert to clutch at his glasses. "So maybe there's a *slight* excuse. But in a year or so you'll be attending *my* school and you'd better understand this now. I do not tolerate this sort of behavior from my students in or *out* of school. And I have a long memory for faces. . . ."

Too late, McGurk started puffing out his cheeks and making his eyes go squinty—what he calls his "Instant Disguise."

"In the meantime, Officer," Mrs. Kelly chipped in, "why don't you book them?"

The air flew out of McGurk's cheeks as if *they'd* been punctured.

Patrolman Cassidy looked at the woman. His face had gotten a deep pink. But his eyes had a cool glint in them.

"Lady," he said, "you may not have noticed this. But your husband is parked on a double yellow line. Your husband is perpetrating a traffic violation."

The woman's mouth sagged open.

"Now, seeing how you're strangers here," the cop went on, "I might overlook it this one time. But if I take the book out for these kids, I have to take it out for your husband. O.K.?"

For once, Mr. Kelly's eyes wavered.

"Uh—thank you, Officer. Quite right. Thank you . . . . Come, Mildred."

He left with a weak smile and a hard, hard look.

The smile was for Patrolman Cassidy. The look was for us.

"Gee, Mr. Cassidy! Thanks!"

The cop gave McGurk a stern glance.

"Don't thank me. Just keep your enthusiasm in check. That guy had every right to be sore. And if you *had* let his air out, there'd have been nothing I could do."

"No," said McGurk, "but you've got to admit it did look suspicious. Car outside bank, engine running."

"Well, it *might* have looked suspicious—back in the old days."

"Huh?"

"Back in the '20s and '30s. In the days of the Dillinger gang, and Machine-Gun Kelly, and—"

"Machine-Gun *Who*?" cried McGurk, giving a little leap of excitement.

"Machine-Gun Kelly. Big bank robber. He—ah!" The cop grinned. "I see what you mean. Even the *name* fits—right?"

All at once, we felt cheered up. Patrolman Cassidy may not have realized it, but it looked like he'd just fixed the new Junior High principal's nickname for years to come. You could almost see McGurk storing it away behind his look of glee.

But then that look faded.

"Why would it have looked suspicious in the old days but not now?"

"Because in those days that's how they used to operate," said the cop. "Getaway car all ready to roll, outside the bank. You've probably seen it in the movies."

"Yes, but—"

"But that was when there wasn't much traffic. Before parking problems got so bad. Nowadays there can't be many downtown banks that don't have double yellow lines outside."

"Yes, sir!" said Brains. "Bank robbers would never risk it, would they?"

"No *smart* bank robber would," said the cop. "Attract police attention by illegal parking? No way!"

McGurk looked tense.

"So—what *do* they do?"

"Why, park in some legal slot, of course. Not necessarily near the bank, either. They usually make their hit at a busy time, when the sidewalks are crowded. Then they slip out and mingle with the crowd."

"You mean just *walk* away?"

"Sure. Probably they slip the loot sack to a member of the gang who never even went into the bank. Then they make their way to the car quietly, singly, without attracting attention."

McGurk was drinking all this in. He'd looked disappointed at first. But gradually the gleam returned to his eyes.

And by the time Mr. Cassidy had gone on his way, McGurk was already starting to make new plans.

"Men!" he said. "Let's get back to HQ. We've got to approach this thing from a whole new angle!"

6 Camera Patrol

"Two things," said McGurk, rocking thoughtfully in his chair. "Now that we know their methods. *Two* new angles."

"Yes," said Wanda. "*One*—we might as well give up and leave it to the real police. And *two*—we better start working on a letter of apology to Mr. and Mrs. Kelly."

The rocking chair jerked faster.

"No *way* do we quit—just because of a little setback! As for the Kellys, the best way to make it right is to prove we really are doing something useful."

"You mean by actually helping to catch some bank robbers?" I said.

"What else?" said McGurk. "You saw the way that guy looked at us. It's the *only* thing that'll convince him."

Wanda sighed. Like the rest of us, she wasn't looking forward to starting a Junior High School career at the head of the principal's black list.

"So what *are* your two angles, McGurk?"

The rocking resumed its normal steady rhythm.

"*One*—the task is a whole lot harder. We'll have to use *all* our powers of observation now." McGurk gave the junk drawer a look of disgust. "Which isn't all that great in some cases. . . ."

"You mean—?"

"I mean we'll have to spot a likely bank robber just by looking at him as he moves around on foot."

"Fat chance!" muttered Brains.

"Oh, yeah? Well, how about my Number *Two* point?" McGurk was smirking. "If it'll be harder for us, then it'll be harder for them, too—working without getaway cars outside the banks."

"How come?"

"A bank robber—" said McGurk, slowly, "your real *professional* bank robber—needs a gun. Right? And not just a small handgun, either. Remember, he's got to scare a whole roomful of people. So— what's he use?"

"A machine gun," said Willie.

"A machine *pistol*," said Brains. "To be technically accurate."

"Or most likely a shotgun," I said. "Sawed-off, probably."

"Right!" said McGurk. "But, sawed-off or not, a gun like that isn't something you can just stick in your pocket while you're walking around the streets. So—"

"Hey, yes!" said Wanda. "So he uses something to carry it in. Something innocent-looking, but big enough—*long* enough. A—a violin case. Or a guitar case."

"Good thinking, Officer Grieg. We keep a sharp eye for people carrying things like that."

"They could just be wearing long coats," said Willie, frowning thoughtfully.

"Huh?"

"Yeah. They could have the guns slung around their necks and hanging down loose in front of them, inside their long coats."

"Come *on*, Willie!" said Wanda. "A shotgun *pendant*?"

"It's true!" said Willie. "I saw it on TV once. That way it leaves their hands free."

We nodded. Even Wanda.

"It would only work in winter, though," she said.
"In summer they'd look pretty suspicious, going
around in long coats."

"It's winter *now*, Officer Grieg," McGurk remind-
ed her. "*Very* good thinking, Officer Sandowsky. . . .
So there we have it, men. That's *also* what we look
for. People with unusually long loose coats."

"When do we start?" said Willie, getting up.

"Sit down! . . . Right after lunch. We'll make the regular patrol but forget about getaway cars. . . . And one more thing." McGurk's eyes had suddenly brightened. "I guess it *was* crazy to think about flinging ourselves at the feet of the robbers. We could get ourselves killed that way."

"It was *your* idea, McGurk."

Ignoring Wanda, McGurk surged on.

"So what we do, we take pictures of them."

"Pictures?"

"Yeah. You have a Polaroid camera, Brains, and I got one for Christmas. Anyone else? . . . Any you can borrow?"

Wanda, Willie and I frowned. We said we'd try.

"Doesn't matter," said McGurk. "Don't waste time on it. Two'll be enough."

Wanda still looked doubtful.

"Just a minute, McGurk. You can't just hang around outside a bank with a camera up to your eye —waiting for someone to come barreling out with a sackful of loot. Besides, you heard what Mr. Cassidy said. They'll probably walk out as cool as if they'd just been cashing a check. How would you *know*?"

McGurk was smiling in that obnoxiously wise way of his.

"We *wouldn't*!" he said. "But if we'd been snapping every person with a violin case or guitar case
or gunny sack or long loose coat—"

"Hey! Yeah!" said Brains. "And then got to hear
of a heist!"

"Which we soon *would*!" I said.

McGurk was nodding, grinning.

52

"Well, *then* we'll be able to show the police the pictures we'd taken only minutes before," he said. "And then they'd have something positive to work with."

We had to hand it to him. It was a great idea.

I could hardly wait to finish my lunch that day— and not just because it was cold turkey again, either!

Once again, our patrol started with a bang. Wanda, Willie and I hadn't been able to borrow any cameras, but that left us free to act as spotters while McGurk and Brains concentrated on taking pictures. The only snag at first was the fact that there were so many long loose coats around. Right away, Brains protested that he'd run out of film soon, and McGurk agreed.

"We'd better stick with *men* in long loose coats. They're more likely to be bank robbers than the women."

Even so, we were kept pretty busy. In the first complete circuit, Brains and McGurk had scored, between them, ten men in such coats, one woman (McGurk had decided after all that she looked hard enough to be a female bank robber), and a kid with a guitar case. In fact, our cameramen were so busy, they had no time to see what they'd taken, and it was left to Wanda and me to hold the pictures, while McGurk and Brains went on snapping away and Willie scouted.

Then, just as we'd passed Bank C, something happened.

"McGurk! Brains! Look! Look!"

Willie was pointing up toward the station. We had already seen the train from New York pull in, and now the passengers were beginning to emerge.

At first I wondered what Willie had seen. Then:

"Wow! Yes!" Wanda murmured. "See them?"

I nodded, gulped, and stared at the group of men and women—all carrying violin cases.

Three, four, *five* of them.

Then another bunch. More instrument cases—some of them bigger—all black and sinister.

"Oh, my gosh!" McGurk murmured, his eyes pop-
ping. "They're coming in *strength*! They've been
squeezed out of New York and now they're *really*
starting on us! It's an *invasion*! They—they're gonna
hold up the whole town!"

"We just don't have enough film!" was all Brains
could say. "What shall we do?"

"Hold it!" I said. "They all seem to be heading
for that bus."

It was near the exit to the station parking lot. I
could see the exhaust fumes and guessed the motor
was already running.

"A—getaway *bus*? said Willie.

"Just a minute!" Wanda drawled. "I think I know
what this might be."

She walked on ahead.

"Be careful, Officer Grieg!" said McGurk. "Don't
let them see we're wise to them."

She was already in front of the bus. We saw her
flick her hair and stare up at the driver. The man
stuck his head out and said something to her.

"We'd better go in support," muttered McGurk.

But just then Wanda turned, and we saw she was
grinning.

"What's so funny?" said McGurk, still with a wary

eye on a new wave of people with instrument cases.

"That!" said Wanda, pointing.

We stared at the printed label pasted across the top of the windshield:

ON CHARTER
TO THE
METROPOLITAN
SYMPHONY
ORCHESTRA

"They're giving a concert at County Hall tonight," said Wanda. "They're on their way there now. They're having a public rehearsal this afternoon."

"Want to come along, kids?" said the driver. "It's free."

"*Yuk!*" went McGurk.

He didn't mean to be ungracious, I could tell. He was just sick to his stomach with disappointment. When I pointed out that it was now after three, the banks' closing time, his expression became gloomier.

"Never mind," said Brains. "There might have been a robbery already. Then our pictures will come in handy after all."

McGurk cheered up a bit at that.

And even when we made one last patrol and saw no signs of such a robbery—no crowd outside any of the banks, no patrol cars pulled up in a bunch, no ambulances—he still didn't fall *all* the way back into despair.

"Oh, well!" he said. "Let's go back and study the pictures. One or two of them *could* have been bank robbers. Maybe they just had to call off today's holdup for some reason."

Some of the pictures were a laugh. I mean if any of those people *had* been bank robbers, the police would have had no help at all.

"You should have taken more care, Officer Bellingham!" growled McGurk.

"*Me? I? You* took those, McGurk!"

"I did *not*!"

"You did *so*! I can tell by the paper. Look. Yours has a different marking on the back."

Brains was right.

Even McGurk couldn't talk his way out of that one. Not against a very indignant science expert.

And Brains had every cause to be miffed.

Here are just two examples of McGurk's photographic skills that afternoon. The first is his picture of the "hard-looking" woman. The second is of the kid with the guitar case.

"Nice shot of the guitar case!" jeered Brains.

"Yes," said Wanda. "I must hand it to you, McGurk. You sure go straight for the essential details. I mean that really *is* a long loose coat the woman's wearing."

"All right!" said McGurk. "Laugh! But let me tell you all something. There's a whole *bunch* of stuff the cops would be able to latch onto. Even in these —uh—slightly out-of-focus shots."

"Like *what*?"

"Well—uh—like the make of boots there. And where the guy had his hair cut. And—uh.... *Anyway*, even those details are better than nothing. Which is what you guys would have come up with if the cops had to rely on your powers of observation alone!"

He glared at us. His rocking became brisker now.

"I mean like for starters—what color was that woman's hair? Huh? . . . How tall was she? What was the guitar guy wearing? What color were his eyes? How tall was *he*?"

We looked at each other, hoping someone would have at least one firm answer. We frowned. We cleared our throats.

And when our *guesses* were offered, they were so feeble that McGurk's self-confidence was fully restored.

"See what I mean?"

For the rest of the afternoon, he put us through session after session of his observation game, using a whole new stock of junk.

By the time he was through, some of us had improved our scores quite a bit. I even managed to get twelve out of fourteen on one round.

But he still wasn't satisfied.

"With *these* tests you've had a warning," he said.

"Yeah! Like thirty seconds a throw!" grumbled Willie (who'd only managed to raise *his* score to six).

McGurk ignored him.

"But tomorrow," he said, "I plan to put you all through a *real* test."

"Like what, McGurk?" Brains asked uneasily. (*Ten* out of fourteen had been *his* best shot.)

"If I told you, you'd be prepared, wouldn't you?"

And nothing we threatened or promised would persuade McGurk to say anything more on the subject.

At first, the next morning, it was the Bank Patrol as usual. We made two complete circuits and Brains and McGurk snapped about a dozen pictures.

This time, though, McGurk took more care. In fact he took so much care he caused quite a stir from time to time. Like when he jostled people on the sidewalk, while he ran ahead to get in a better position to photograph a suspect. Or when he stepped back suddenly onto people's toes.

But this was nothing to the stir he was about to
make!

We'd become so interested that we'd forgotten
all about his threatened mystery test. And even
when he stopped outside Bank A and said, "Come
on! Let's take a look inside!"—even then we didn't
suspect anything but just another of McGurk's crazy
impulses.

"*Inside,* McGurk?" said Wanda. "They'll throw us out!"

"Oh no, they won't!" said McGurk. "This is my father's bank. I'm known here. If anyone asks, we've come to inquire if it's possible for kids to open a savings account on their own."

"But *why*?"

"Why *not*? If we're on a Red Bank-Robber Alert we have to make ourselves familiar with the layout inside the banks we're patrolling, don't we? Sure, we'll go inside. And when we're through here, we'll do the same with every other bank."

Well, this one was *his* father's bank, not mine. And, after all, it did sound reasonable.

So, with McGurk leading the way, we went in.

7 Trouble at the Bank

This is where I get to feel like a stage magician.

First, you have to know that I had never been in that bank before.

Second, we were in there for no more than fifteen minutes.

Third, we were almost immediately caught up in some very personal, very urgent business.

Fourth I have never been in that bank since. (And I don't intend to, either!)

Yet I can give you the exact layout of the front area. And I can tell you, almost exactly, how many people were in there when we entered, and just where each one of them was standing or sitting.

For starters, here is my drawing of the layout:

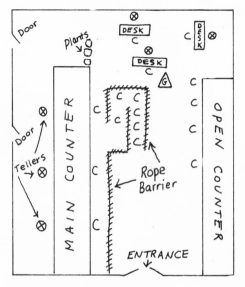

As you see, there were sixteen customers. Three of these were at the main counter. Six were lined up behind the ropes, waiting their turn. Three were sitting in front of the three desks at the far end, discussing business with the assistant managers. And four were standing by the long narrow open counter at the side, writing out checks or studying the leaflets or whatever.

I have already mentioned six of the staff members: the three tellers and the other three at their desks. That leaves the guard: a tall gray-haired man, whose back was turned when we entered. He was saying something to the executive at the first desk.

So—how come I can be so accurate?

Does the Great Rokawi have a split-second photographic memory?

Has he learned some secret method from the monks of Tibet—a method that gives him supernatural powers of observation?

The answer to all these questions is: *No, no chance.*

There is no magic solution. I, plain Joey Rockaway, freely admit that I had scarcely even *started* to look around, when we entered that bank.

In fact I only had eyes for McGurk at that point.

He'd suddenly come to a stop after taking about three steps. We others were bunched up behind him and he'd made us bump into each other. At first I thought he was wondering whether to get in line behind the ropes or head straight for the desks.

But then I saw he wasn't looking around at all. He was looking *down*. At his camera. *While he fiddled around with a flash cube!*

"Hey!" I gasped. "McGurk! You're not thinking of—?"

But he was.

And while I spoke, he did it.

He lifted the camera, peered through the viewfinder—and pushed the button.

There was a flash.

Not a flash coupled with an explosion.

Just an ordinary camera flashbulb flash.

But coming out of the blue in such a place as that, it might just as well have been a flash of lightning or high explosive.

Now, other people had been reading about the possibility of a wave of bank robberies, too, remember. It must have been a scary thought at the back of their minds.

So, almost at the same instant as the flash, there was a scream. And, almost at the same instant as the scream, someone must have pressed a button. An alarm bell started ringing.

Then came the guard's voice, as he whirled around.

"Hold it!" he hollered.

Now *he* must have had quick powers of observation, with reflexes to match. Especially for an old guy.

Because, although his hand had flown to his gun, he didn't draw it. His "Hold it!" was addressed to the panicky customers and staff, not to any imagined holdup man.

"*Hold it, folks!*" he repeated. "*It's only some dumb kid with a camera!*"

And *that* is how I came to know so well just how many people there were in there, plus their locations, plus the general layout. There was no Great Rokawi with a split-second photographic memory.

There was just plain Joey Rockaway's pal McGurk, with a split-second Polaroid camera.

Naturally, there was no time to look at the resulting snapshot right then and there. The guard was bearing down on us at the same time as he was pacifying the customers. And the manager was coming around from somewhere behind the plants at the far end.

As for McGurk, he was saying:

"Sorry! Sorry! Sorry! It just went off by accident. I'd been taking some pictures outside and—"

"Never mind *that!*" snarled the manager, a big man with a bald head and a fierce black moustache. "What are you doing here anyway?" He turned to glance at the customers. "Who are you *with?*" he asked, in a slightly less angry tone.

"Nobody, sir," said McGurk. Then he hurried on when the manager's eyes started to blaze again. "My name's McGurk. Jack P. McGurk. My father's a customer here. Mr. Ray McGurk. Raymond T. McGurk."

"So?" growled the manager—though once again he'd softened his tone up some.

"So I was coming in to inquire if it was possible to open up a savings account without—"

"*Everything O.K.?*"

We turned.

Patrolman Cassidy and another cop had just come in, backs against the sides of the doorway, guns half-drawn.

"Fine, Officer!" said the manager. "It was a false alarm. One of these children happened to set off a flashbulb by accident. . . ."

He even managed a quick smile as he patted McGurk's shoulder. Just a flash of teeth under the moustache—but a definite smile. Either the manager was a very kindly man, I thought, or Mr. McGurk was a very good customer!

Mr. Cassidy did *not* smile. He kept his expression grave. His partner, a red-faced man with suspicious little eyes, took it one stage further. He swept us all with a big dark scowl.

"I see," said Patrolman Cassidy, holstering his gun. "I'll have a word with you later, young M'Turk!"

"*McGurk*, Mr. Cassidy!" said our leader. He spoke anxiously. I could guess why. Mr. Cassidy was always getting his name wrong, and McGurk was used to that. But right now he didn't want that manager to be in any doubt. "The name's *McGurk*."

"Sure!" said Mr. Cassidy, still looking very grim. He turned to his partner. "Let's go, Don."

The manager dealt with McGurk's query personally. Probably he was letting McGurk go out of turn. But that guy had the look of someone who wanted to get rid of someone else pretty fast, before that someone else could cause any more trouble. McGurk often has that effect on adults.

So, in two minutes flat, we were being steered to the door, with the manager saying, "The best thing would be for you to ask your father to make the arrangements. But since you want to keep it a secret from him—"

"You *bet*, sir!" said McGurk, stopping in his tracks. "Absolute secrecy! I want to surprise him with it. When—when I've saved twenty dollars."

"Sure! Sure!" The manager resumed his steering. "So why don't I mail you personally—Master Jack P. McGurk—the leaflets outlining our different plans."

McGurk wasn't really interested, of course—once he'd made sure his father wasn't going to hear of this. And as soon as we were out on the sidewalk, he said triumphantly:

"Right, men! Now I have a *real* test for you. Exactly who was in the bank at the time of the flash? Exactly where were they standing or sitting? We now have a photographic record to check your answers against. We'll go right back to HQ and—"

But we weren't going anywhere right away.

"The Red Bank-Robber Alert again?"

It was Mr. Cassidy.

Still grave. Still very grim.

"Uh—yes—yes, sir!" said McGurk. "We—I was taking this picture for training. A—uh—*training film.* And—"

"And that's the end of it!" said Mr. Cassidy, in a low but very penetrating voice. "Finish. No more. The end. O.K.?" He bent a little and held his face closer to McGurk's. "Do you realize how serious that could have been?"

"I think *I* do, sir," Brains began. "But he never mentioned it to—"

"I'm talking to McCork here," said Mr. Cassidy, without taking his eyes off McGurk's. Our leader gulped and shot Brains an angry glance. "Do you have *any* idea," Patrolman Cassidy went on, "what might have happened if that guard in there had been a bit confused or trigger-happy?"

McGurk's face got redder. He lowered his eyes.

"And do you realize what Lieutenant Kaspar would say—and *do*—if this ever got back to him?. . ."

Mr. Cassidy went on like that for about ten minutes. He never raised his voice. But also he

never repeated himself. He'd had lots of experience in getting points across to kids. And when he was through, even McGurk was convinced.

"So—no more Bank Patrols, M'Quirk. Right?"

"Y—yes, Mr. Cassidy. I mean no. No more Bank Patrols, sir."

"I got your word?"

"Yes, sir."

"All of you?"

We gave it. Gladly.

"Right!" said Patrolman Cassidy, tipping his cap and straightening up.

We went back to HQ in a much quieter mood than when we'd started.

We'd been ordered off cases before, but never in such a manner as that. And this time there was no arguing.

Mr. Cassidy had been absolutely right.

If that guard had not been so good at his job, there could have been mayhem in there!

"Anyway," muttered McGurk, as we reached his basement steps, "we can still have a good training session with the picture."

He didn't realize it, of course—but that picture was going to get us into something much more dramatic than any training session.

8 A Very Special Visitor

"The camera flash was a warning shot. After that, it was everybody face down on the floor. So write down exactly how many people were in there at the time of the flash. And their exact locations."

That was the test question McGurk gave us to work on. And this time he was very generous, allowing us a full half-hour to write our answers.

Naturally, some of us had been thinking about it a whole lot longer than that. Ever since McGurk had first mentioned the test out in the street, in fact.

But it didn't help much.

The results were so bad that I'm too ashamed to

give them here. The closest anyone got to the number of people was Willie. He said thirty, but he was honest enough to admit that it was a guess.

"I just knew there was a *crowd.* You know—something bigger than just a *bunch.* And I always figure a crowd at around thirty. Same size as a class at school. Sort of."

But as for giving the location of each person, his guesses were no better than anyone else's.

"Terrible!" said McGurk, when he compared our answers to the picture. "You get *worse!*"

"This afternoon, McGurk," said Wanda, "I am going to borrow Brains's camera and *I'll* snap a crowd scene and then we'll see how good *your* score is!"

"Fine!" said McGurk. "You do that, Officer Grieg. I'll be glad to show you what a *really* keen observer can do."

"Oh sure!" said Brains. "Now that you've been alerted."

"But in the meantime," said McGurk, laying the picture down but keeping his hand over it, "I'll see what you can do when you *are* alerted." He looked at his watch. "You have exactly thirty seconds, men, to study the picture and refresh your lousy memories. Starting . . . *now!*"

Then he took his hand away and we bent our heads and started to refresh those lousy memories.

Well, the picture wasn't all that good. I mean it didn't cover all the area I drew in the plan. But it did show most of the customers lining up behind the ropes, and all of those at the long counter on the right. This made it easier to fill in the gaps— like remembering how many tellers there were, and who was sitting at the desks.

So the results were a lot better, this time, even though we were still unable to agree about just how many people there *were* in those gaps.

"I say there were *two* tellers!"

"And I say *three!*"

"You're both wrong. There were *four!*"

And so on, and on, and on.

In fact we might have continued arguing for hours, if there hadn't been the knock on the door.

"See who it is, Officer Rockaway," growled Mc-Gurk. "That is, if you can remember where the door is located."

(He was mad because I'd been the one to say three tellers while he'd insisted on two—and I think it was beginning to dawn on him that I'd been right.)

I opened the door.

"Hi!" said the man standing there. "So this is the
headquarters of the famous McGurk Organization!"

He was very tall and heavily built. I guess he
looked bulkier because of the way he was muffled
up: thick overcoat, red woolen scarf, fur hat with
earflaps—and a beard.

To me, big men always look bigger when they wear beards. Even if they're only short squared-off beards like his. Color of beard (just to prove *I don't* go around with my eyes half-shut): a sandy medium brown.

"My name's Mark Westover," he said. "I'm a reporter with the *Evening Gazette and Advertiser*. May I—?"

"Sure! Sure! Mr. Westover!" This was McGurk, who'd come bustling around as soon as the word *reporter* had been mentioned. "Step right in."

I was still gazing at the card the man had handed me. As the official ID-card designer for the Organization, I was thinking the *Gazette* could use someone with my talents. This card was just an ordinary piece of pasteboard, quite small. Here is a copy:

```
┌─────────────────────────────────┐
│          MARK WESTOVER          │
│     Human Interest Reporter     │
│                                 │
│    Evening Gazette & Advertiser │
│                                 │
└─────────────────────────────────┘
```

"Thank you," said the man, taking it from me and slipping it back into his pocket. "And now that you've seen my credentials, maybe you can guess why I'm here."

Well, *I* couldn't. But before anyone had time to make a suggestion, the reporter was explaining.

"I heard about the mix-up in the bank a couple of hours ago," he said. His beard wagged as he laughed softly. "And I thought it might make an amusing story." He laughed again. "You sure must have thrown a scare into those people. . . . Is that the camera?"

McGurk nodded. He reached for the camera and held it out, but the man wasn't all that interested. He was too busy looking around.

"So *why?*" he said, turning back to McGurk. "Why take pictures in a bank anyway? That's the first thing my readers will want to know."

McGurk's face was a picture. His freckles were shifting all over the place as he frowned and squirmed and grinned and bit his lips.

I could tell what was going through his mind.

If the story appeared in the newspaper, his father would be sure to hear of it.

But if the story didn't appear, the Organization would lose all that free publicity.

Furthermore, if McGurk stuck to his excuse that the flashbulb went off by accident, the reporter might decide it wasn't worth writing about after all.

On the other hand, if McGurk told the whole truth, the reporter would certainly find it unusual enough to print—*in which case McGurk wouldn't be able to fall back on the "accident" excuse when his father questioned him.*

Well, it didn't take him long to choose.

"Let me tell you about it, Mr. Westover," he began. "As you know, we're a detective agency. And because detectives have to be keen and alert and sharp-eyed at all times. . . ."

He went on to explain his idea for the test.

"I see," said the man, scribbling something down in his notebook. (A brand-new one, exactly the same type as the ones I use, I was pleased to see.) "And you chose a bank because—"

"Because we're on Red Bank-Robbery Alert. Yes, sir!"

"I was the one who read about it in your paper," said Brains. "About how the bank robbers in New York—"

"And *your* name is—?"

Brains told him. Then the man made notes of all our names.

"Show him your ID cards, men!" said McGurk.

We produced the cards, but the reporter seemed

more interested in the files, the typewriter, the copying machine and the handcuffs. Especially the last two.

As we explained how we came to have these things, he scribbled away faster.

"Fascinating!" he kept muttering. "Will our readers love *this!*"

Finally, he glanced at his watch and gave a start.

"I'd better be going," he said. "If I'm going to make tonight's main edition."

A kind of stir of excitement went among us. We could almost see the headline in the paper: YOUNG DETECTIVES SHAKE BANK CUSTOMERS.

"Oh, and by the way!" The man laughed and slapped his forehead. "The most important item of all. The picture you took. Did it turn out O.K.? Like show the startled expressions on their faces?"

"Here, sir," said McGurk, his face glowing as he handed the picture over. "See for yourself."

The reported scrutinized it, frowning slightly.

"Hm!" he said. "Not bad. . . . A little retouching here and there . . . and it could reproduce pretty well . . . yeah."

"You mean you'd like to use it in the paper?" said Wanda.

"Sure! Why not? It's what the fuss was all about."

The man turned to McGurk. "Is this the only one
you took in the bank? I mean you wouldn't have
another, clearer one, would you?"

"No, sir. Just that." McGurk was looking anxious,
like he wished he'd taken a bit more trouble over
the focusing. "But you're welcome to use it, if you
think—"

"Sure! No problem. Like I said, we can have it
touched up." He glanced at his watch again. "I'd
better go." He put the picture carefully inside his
notebook. "I'll see that you get this back."

He stopped on his way to the door. He pointed to the copying machine.

"You didn't by any chance make a few copies on *that*, did you?"

"No," said McGurk. "But now you mention it, sir, maybe Joey here could do that right now."

He gave me a glare—obviously mad because I hadn't thought of it before.

"Don't bother," said the man. "No time. And anyway, we won't keep this for long. I'll bring it back personally, when I come with *our* photographer."

"*Your* photographer?" said Wanda. "The—the *Gazette*'s?"

"Sure!" said the man. "To take *your* pictures. And —uh—some shots of your HQ. . . . But first we'll get *this* story in because of its news value. Like I said, we'll try and make tonight's edition—if not, then tomorrow's. *Then* we'll follow up in our weekend magazine section. With a full in-depth article about The McGurk Organization. O.K.?"

Again the thrill of excitement had gone through us.

I mean—a full-length article! With pictures!

McGurk had turned quite white.

"*Sure!* . . . Uh—sir?"

"Yes?"

"When will you be coming with the photographer?"

The man frowned.

"Uh—I'll try for this afternoon. Will you all be here?"

"You bet!"

"Otherwise sometime tomorrow. Probably morning. I'll be in touch."

When he'd gone, there was a long purring sort of silence.

Then McGurk broke it with a clap of his hands.

"Right, men! You heard what he said. This weekend article is our big chance to prove to Machine-Gun Kelly that we really are serious. So I want you all back here right after lunch. *In your best clothes!*"

Press Photographer

9 The Holdup

The McGurk Organization had never looked so spiffy as it did that afternoon. McGurk, Willie, Brains and I were all wearing suits. Even Wanda had left her old flowered jeans at home and had turned up in a new red velvet dress.

But it was all wasted as far as having our photographs taken for a magazine article was concerned. In fact it would have been a *total* waste if Mrs. McGurk hadn't come down around 3:30 with a huge tray loaded with goodies.

"I wish you'd told me earlier you were having an Organization Christmas Party, Jack," she said. "You'd better come up and get the Cokes yourself."

"Christmas P—?" Willie began, until McGurk
stepped on the toes of his shiny new loafers.
As McGurk explained
later, he'd had to
account for borrowing
one of his father's best
silk neckties. Naturally,
he hadn't wanted to
tell his mother about
the reporter—not
before the article
appeared. "So I said
we were having a sort
of Christmas Party."

Well, it was a consolation. Mrs. McGurk hadn't
done so badly on such short notice. Personally, I
could have done without the turkey sandwiches,
but the potato chips and the cheese straws and the
brownies were quite delicious. There was even a
new kind of party game. I guess it could be called
"*Save Some for the Visitors.*" As McGurk pointed out:

"You *could* call it a special training-session game.
Testing your will power. All detectives should have
iron will power."

Unfortunately, that was still another test we

failed. Chip by chip, brownie by brownie, cheese straw by cheese straw, we nibbled through the small stock we'd set aside for the reporter and photographer. By 4:30, there were only two rather dry turkey sandwiches and one can of Coke left.

"I never really expected them to make it this afternoon, anyway," said McGurk (who'd been responsible for quite a bit of this extra nibbling). "No," he said, reaching for one of the remaining sandwiches, "what I'm really looking forward to *today* is seeing the bank story in tonight's *Gazette*. Brains?"

Brains had already told us how his parents had the evening paper delivered regularly. It usually came between 4:30 and 5:30.

"I'll go see," he said. "It's still a bit early, but. . . ."

But he might have saved himself the trouble.

Oh, yes, the paper *had* arrived! And oh yes, his mother *did* allow him to snatch it up and run all the way back to our HQ with it!

But there was no bank mix-up story.

We went through that paper page by page and column by column. We checked and double-checked.

Then we started trying to look on the bright side.

"Oh, well," said McGurk, "he did say it was a bit late for tonight's edition."

"Sure," said Brains. "I always figured it wouldn't be in until tomorrow."

"And it isn't as if we have to wait a whole twenty-four hours," I pointed out. "Don't forget we can get a copy of the early edition ourselves, if we go downtown, just after lunch."

"My guess is we won't need to," said Wanda. "Mr. Westover will bring an advance copy with him, when he comes to interview us tomorrow morning."

McGurk was so cheered up by this that he reached for the last sandwich. By way of celebration, I suppose.

"Be here early, men," he said. "Best clothes, remember!"

It was practically the same routine all over again, that Friday morning. All that was missing was another tray of goodies. McGurk's excuse for dressing up this time was that he'd decided to hold an Annual General Meeting of the Organization. His mother, knowing him of old, had seen through this —but hadn't been so good with her second guessing.

"If you think that simply by wearing your best clothes you can trick me into catering another basement party, you're mistaken," she said. "Besides, I'll be out all morning, marketing."

Well, we didn't mind that. It meant there'd be less danger of her stumbling into the interview, asking awkward questions.

So we spent the time setting up our equipment: polishing the handcuffs, tidying the files, and generally making sure there'd be plenty of interesting material for the *Gazette* people to write about and photograph.

And again—zilch.

This time, McGurk didn't take it so well.

At 12:30 he dragged off his father's necktie, flung it clear across the table and said bitterly:

"That's it, then! We've been stood up!"

We nodded. Most of us had lost hope over an hour ago.

"He *could* be busy on some other project," murmured Wanda. "Something urgent that's come up. I—I *guess*."

"*Morning!*" growled McGurk. "He definitely said this *morning!* If he couldn't make it yesterday afternoon, it would be this *morning!*"

"Well, never mind, McGurk," I said. "It's almost time for today's early edition to hit the newsstands downtown. Soon we'll be able to read about the bank story."

That brought the glimmer back to his eyes.

"Hey, yeah! I forgot about that. Go grab some lunch, men, and make it snappy. I want you all back at one o'clock."

By 1:15, we were on our way downtown. McGurk was looking strained and somewhat miffed. He was still wearing his best suit, whereas the rest of us had changed back into our regular comfortable clothes. He hadn't liked that.

"As soon as we pick up the paper, I want us all back at HQ, in case he decides to make it this afternoon. And what happens? You turn up looking like a bunch of scarecrows!"

"But you said yourself if he didn't show this morning he wouldn't be coming at all!" said Wanda. "We can't be hanging around in your basement in our best clothes for the rest of our *lives!*"

"Yeah!" grumbled Willie. "That's what—"

"Argh, be quiet!" snapped McGurk.

We'd reached the newsstand by then. He'd already picked up and paid for a copy of that day's *Gazette.*

We crowded around him on the cold sidewalk as he slowly turned the pages—muttering.

Gradually, the muttering grew to a groaning, and the groaning into a final howl of anger that caused passers-by to look around in alarm.

"He's forgotten us! The jerk's gone and forgotten us!"

"McGurk!" muttered Wanda. "Keep your voice down!"

"But we'll see about this!" snarled McGurk. "We'll see about this right now!"

In his anger, he had compressed the paper into a crumpled ball.

"See about it *how?*" I said.

"We're going straight to the *Gazette* office!" said McGurk.

There was no arguing with him in that mood. So we followed him in a silent bunch as he strode down to the corner of Main and West Willow and into the *Gazette* front office.

"Yeah?" said the man behind the counter, through a wreath of cigar smoke. "What can I do for ya?"

He wasn't very tall—but he was very wide. His bald head was marked with several small blue scars, like he'd used it to hammer nails with. Tough, anyway.

McGurk blinked. His own fierce expression softened. He even attempted one of his squirming grins.

"Sorry to trouble you, sir—"

"Maybe ya will be, at that!"

"But—uh—could we speak with Mr. Westover, sir? Mr. Mark Westover?"

The man blew another cloud of smoke.

"Who wants him? And why?"

Stumbling over his words at first, but gradually getting more fluent as his indignation returned, McGurk explained about our visitor.

"Well, now," said the man, when McGurk had finished, "this all sounds very, very fishy to me."

"Sir?"

"Yeah. Because for one thing"—he stabbed another cloud of smoke with his cigar—"Mark Westover wouldn't *touch* a story like that. And for another thing"—another stab—"Mark Westover happens to be on vacation all this week." Stab again. "In *Hawaii*. . . . But now you got me interested. What did this guy look like?"

We told him.

He shook his head.

"Couldn't be one of the others, then. No one with a beard on this staff. You sure he said the *Gazette*?"

"Not only that—he showed us his card," I said.

"His *press* card? And it had Mark Westover's *name and picture* on it?"

All at once, I felt like kicking myself. I'd *sensed* there'd been something wrong about that card!

"No, sir. . . ."

I described it.

He gave a short barking laugh.

"*That* was no press card! A press card it says PRESS—in big letters even dumb cops can read. And there's *always* a picture of the holder." The man frowned. "From the way you describe it, that card was a phony. One of these Print-Your-Own-Calling-

Cards jobs. You can buy a cheap kit in almost any stationers. Like at Steins, across the street."

McGurk gave me a glare. Stationery is *my* department. As if *I* could have known!

"So—so you think we've been tricked, sir?" he said.

"Sure of it," murmured the man. He was frowning thoughtfully as he flicked some ash onto the counter. Then he swept it off with a big hairy hand, looked up and said: "What bugs me, son, is *why*."

McGurk nodded. His eyes had an angry glint.

"Yeah. Me, too!"

"Your folks don't happen to have any valuables laying around the house, do they?" asked the man. "I mean *really* valuable valuables? The sort of stuff a certain type of guy might get to hear about and— excuse me."

The ringing of the phone had cut through our gasps.

We waited impatiently—eager now to hear more about his theory.

But he never got around to it.

"*What?!*" he bellowed into the receiver." You mean this branch *here*? On Main Street? . . . When? . . . No! I'll cover this one myself! . . . *Jane!*"

A girl came running from the back, wiping crumbs from her mouth.

"Sorry about this!" he told her, already moving toward the door. "You'll just have to finish your lunch out here." He was hitching on a coat at the open door." There's been a bank holdup. Five minutes ago. The one near the corner of Main and Elm. . . . *Hah!*" He directed at us one last jab of his cigar. "*Your* bank! The one you were just telling me about!"

Then he was off—out into the streets that were already filled with wailing and screaming sirens—leaving us gaping at one another.

10 The Bashful Bank Robber?

It didn't take us long to get to the bank.

This time there was a crowd—growing bigger every second. And this time there *were* patrol cars pulled up outside—four of them, two on either side, forming a barrier outside the bank entrance to help keep the crowd back.

There was no ambulance, though. At least, not yet.

We'd already seen Patrolman Cassidy controlling the traffic farther down Main Street. There was another cop in the middle of the road outside the bank doing the same. The traffic was slowed to a crawl for three reasons: (1) because of the single-lane bottleneck outside the bank; (2) because of drivers rubbernecking; and (3) because already road blocks had been set up in the downtown area, causing jams.

We found out about Number 3 later. We also found out that it hadn't done any good. The robbers must have parked their car some distance away —strategically placed to slip out of such a roadblock net.

We pushed to the front of the crowd until we came within touching distance of one of the patrol cars. There we were kept back by one of the cops. Another was on duty at the door of the bank, questioning our friend from the *Gazette*. After the man had produced his press card, however, he was allowed in.

"Let's find out what happened," said McGurk. "Come on, men! Ask around."

Well, there were plenty of people there ready to give their *ideas* about what had happened. Here's a selection just as I jotted them down:

Holdup Details (according to Bystanders)
- 12 armed men
- 3 armed men
- All wearing ski masks.
- All wearing Mickey Mouse masks.
- Guard and 2 tellers shot dead.
- No dead - 7 injured.
- $800,000 haul.
- $50,000
- $1,000 only.

As I say, that was only a selection. And as far as containing any real information—let alone *evidence* —is concerned, you can forget it.

In fact here is my report on the facts, which I made for our case files after it was all over:

DETAILS OF HOLDUP AS IT REALLY
HAPPENED (BASED ON OFFICIAL
POLICE & FBI INFORMATION, & LATER
NEWS REPORTS.)

1:45 P.M. Two men in ski masks enter bank. (Must have been wearing them as caps earlier and pulled them down over faces when through the door.)

Immediately produce sawed-off shotguns. One aimed at guard; the other at elderly woman customer.

1st Robber's exact words: "Everyone do as we say or this lady gets blown in half."

2nd Robber's exact words: "That goes for if anyone sets off any secret alarm."

Results: (1) Guard even less likely to take action; (2) Everyone else less likely to panic (since gun not directed at *them* personally).

1:47 P.M. Man with gun aimed at guard disarms him and goes behind main counter, with new large black plastic garbage sack.

1:48 (and at various times later). Man with lady hostage at side of door warns every newcomer who enters: "Go straight on in and stand by those desks over there. This is a stickup, but nobody will get hurt if—" etc. etc.

1:55. Man with sack (now filled with nearly $90,000 in used bills) joins man at door. *Last warning:* "We're taking this lady with us as far as the car. Anyone raises alarm before that clock says 2:00, she'll get wasted."

Men turn, woman between them. Guns under coats. Masks off at door (while backs turned to people inside). They go nice and casually into street.

1st Conclusion. So the three robbers had a good head start and could get out and mingle with passers-by.

Questions and Answers.

Q. *Three* robbers?
A. Oh, yes! You see, the little old lady hostage wasn't an ordinary customer at all. So there was no problem with *her* outside, like if she was to get hysterical. *She* was one of the gang.

Q. *(This question first asked by Officer G. "Brains" Bellingham of The McGurk Organization.)* Didn't the bank have any hidden cameras?
A. Yes. But the pictures were useless. The woman was well-disguised in a natural kind of way (i.e., with wig, different clothes from her usual ones, plus different make-up). The men: their faces were covered with ski masks at all times. Their clothes, too, were probably different from usual ones.

2nd Conclusion. Of course, they'd planned it well. They had cased the bank thoroughly and knew (for instance) exactly where the cameras were placed. In fact it was so well-planned it came pretty close to being a perfect crime. *Which is why our contribution to solving it turned out to be so vital!*

But right at that moment, as we stood with the crowd on Main Street, we had no idea what our contribution would or could be.

McGurk had ideas of what it *might have been*, though.

"If it hadn't been for that phony reporter," he

said bitterly, "we might have been out on patrol with our cameras."

"What? After giving our word to Mr. Cassidy that we *wouldn't* go out on patrol any more?" said Wanda.

McGurk shrugged.

"Well—we might—uh—just have *happened* to be passing."

"Anyway," said Brains, "I'd still like to know why an adult should go to all that trouble, just to fool *us*."

Willie sniffed.

"You heard what that fella in the *Gazette* office was starting to say. Maybe the guy was casing our HQ. Taking a good look—seeing what to steal."

"Huh!" grunted Wanda. "What *is* there to steal? Besides—"

"HEY! WAIT! WAIT JUST ONE SECOND!"

McGurk was jumping up and down. Curious faces were turned. Nothing much was happening outside the bank, and the crowd was hungry for any new development. Even a red-headed freckle-faced kid throwing some kind of fit.

McGurk quieted down and motioned us to get closer.

"No! Listen! Maybe the phony reporter *was* doing some casing! But not at our HQ."

"Huh?"

McGurk was leering now.

"I mean maybe he was casing the bank here!"

"Talk sense, McGurk!" said Wanda. "Why come to our HQ to case a *bank?*"

"No! No!" said McGurk, shaking his head, still leering—thoroughly enjoying himself again. "Don't you *see*? Maybe he was in there when I was taking the flash picture yesterday. Maybe he realized he'd be *in* it. With the risk of being identified later. So he was bashful and wanted it destroyed. Very bashful. The Bashful Bank Robber!"

We stared. He'd got us hanging on every word now.

I decided to make it just a *bit* tougher for him. Anything to take that cocky obnoxious grin off his face.

"But how would he know where to find us?"

McGurk laughed.

"Because I gave out my name enough times, didn't I? To the manager. Loud and clear. All the robber would have to do is look it up in the phone book."

"Of course!" murmured Wanda. "You even came out with your *father's* full name!"

"Hold it!" said Brains, frowning. "Aren't you forgetting something?"

"Like what?"

"Well, wouldn't he be scared of coming to our HQ like that and letting us get a good look at him? Wouldn't it have been better to risk it and hope we wouldn't connect our photograph with what happened today in the bank?"

"He wouldn't worry about *us* identifying him. Not if he came in a *disguise*," said McGurk. "Huh? I mean, take that beard. Even if he didn't use a phony beard as a regular thing, he could easily have gotten one at one of the toy stores here."

"*Hey! YEAH!*" This time it was Willie's turn to make some of the bystanders stare. "There was a

smell. Besides his aftershave—I mean that was a *really* unusual perfume—"

"Oh?" said Wanda. "*I* don't recall—"

"You don't have Willie's special nose!" said McGurk. "Go on, Officer Sandowsky. This smell. Besides the aftershave—"

"Yeah, well, I did catch a whiff of gum. The sticky type gum, I mean. Not chewing gum. When he bent down near me to take a closer look at the copying machine."

"*There* you are!" cried McGurk. "That's *it!* We can give the cops a good description of *one* of the robbers."

"Or of one of the robbers' *disguises*," said Wanda, doubtfully.

But McGurk was already shouldering his way up to the nearest patrolman.

11 The Detailed Description

McGurk struck out twice in the next five minutes.

The first time was with the patrolman.

"But, sir, we've *seen* one of the robbers!"

That caused the officer to take a more careful look at us.

"You mean you were *here*, when the perpetrators came out of the bank?"

"No," said McGurk. "It was yesterday, back home. This guy came to see us—"

"Beat it!" growled the cop.

And that was Strike One.

McGurk was just about to start an argument, when Patrolman Cassidy arrived. The traffic was starting to flow more smoothly now.

"Mr. Cassidy!" said McGurk. "*You* know us. *You* know we don't fool around—"

"Do I?"

The friendly policeman's voice was edged with sarcasm, but his look was serious enough. And when McGurk started to tell him about the phony visitor, and the photograph, and our theory, his face got even more serious.

"What did he look like, this guy?"

"Well, he had a beard, but the beard was a fake. Willie smelled the gum—"

"And the aftershave," Willie chimed in. "A very peculiar—"

"STOP!"

Mr. Cassidy was beginning to look as annoyed as the first cop.

"You think I can take you in there, where Lieutenant Kaspar is busy with a detective squad, taking statements from people who've actually seen the robbers *in action?* You think I can say, 'Drop everything, sir. These kids met this guy with a fake beard yesterday and think he's one of the perpetrators. They don't have an *exact* description, on account of the beard, but they sure got a good whiff of his aftershave.'?"

Strike Two.

Even McGurk had lost some of his confidence by now.

But then Mr. Cassidy showed what a really true friend and a really shrewd cop he was.

"Listen, McGinty—and you others. I'm not trying to put you down. I know you mean well. I even think you might have something there. But there's a time and place for everything—and it isn't *now* and it isn't *here*."

He scratched his chin thoughtfully.

"Sir?"

McGurk's fingers were crossed on both hands.

"Tell you what I'll do," said the cop. "If the robbers haven't been apprehended in the road blocks, I'll *prepare* Lieutenant Kaspar.When he's through in there."

He looked at his watch.

"Why don't you stop by at Police Headquarters at 4:30?"

"But—"

"By *that* time," Mr. Cassidy continued, "the lieutenant should be in a better frame of mind. And also by that time, you will have been able to go over, very carefully, just what you can recall about the guy. Exact details."

We nodded. This was making sense.

"And take a tip from an old cop," Mr. Cassidy went on. "Don't try *each one of you* to give a full head-to-toe description. No. Just try to remember one detail you can each be absolutely sure of."

"Yeah, like the aftershave—" Willie began.

"Now *that*," said the cop, doubtfully, "I wouldn't know about. I mean like how *can* you give an accurate, scientific, pin-point description of a smell? A description that would mean something to another person?"

"Don't worry about that, sir!" said Brains, suddenly flushing. "I've been working on just that problem for a few days now, and I think I have the answer."

"Well, O.K.," said the cop. "So long as it makes sense and doesn't cause the lieutenant to blow his top."

The 4:30 appointment left us with just over an hour and forty-five minutes to go back to our own HQ and get our statement ready. And, believe me, we could have used twice that amount of time.

McGurk didn't help at first. He wasted a good ten minutes bawling out Brains for keeping his scientific smell-recording theory to himself. But when Brains had run off home and returned breathless with his materials, and explained exactly what he'd had in mind, we were all given such a boost in spirits (McGurk included) that it made our own struggles to remember exact details a whole lot easier.

And at 4:35, when we were shown into Lieutenant Kaspar's office, we were really well-equipped.

"So," said the lieutenant, getting straight to the point, "you think you have some information?"

His normally pink face looked pale and strained. Only his eyes had their usual look: bright, clear, blue—and hard.

All at once, I felt gladder than ever that we'd taken Mr. Cassidy's advice.

"Yes, sir," said McGurk.

"These are the kids I was telling you about, Hedley," the lieutenant said to a man who'd been standing at the window, looking out.

The man turned. He wore a dark business suit and rimless glasses. His hair was gray. He looked very grave. I thought he was probably one of the bank officials—until Lieutenant Kaspar introduced him.

"This is Special Agent Hedley Willis of the FBI Bank Detail. He's working with us."

McGurk stiffened. His hand went up to his father's necktie and straightened it. He and the agent were easily the two neatest and best-dressed persons in that office. I could almost *see* the fact going to Mc-Gurk's head. I groaned inwardly. If that was how real FBI men dressed, it looked like The McGurk Organization would soon be getting hit with a strict dress code!

But McGurk didn't allow any of this to throw him off the track. He gave the two men a clear and fairly crisp account of what had happened—leaving out such items as our brush with "Machine-Gun Kelly" and going lightly over the ruckus *we* caused at the bank.

The lieutenant glanced from time to time at the FBI man. I guess he was wondering if he'd better explain just how reliable our help had been in the past—in case the stranger thought we were a bunch of nuts.

But Mr. Willis couldn't have treated our story more seriously.

"So you think you might be able to describe this man?" he said, when McGurk had filled in the background.

"Sure thing, sir!" said McGurk. He smoothed the

lapels of his suit. "I figured we'd best be able to help by concentrating on one certain, exact, hard detail each."

"McGurk!" said Wanda, in a shocked whisper. "That was Mr. Cassidy's idea!"

But neither of the men seemed to hear her.

"Go on," said Lieutenant Kaspar.

"Well first, his height. We left that to Officer Grieg here. She's good at heights. Officer Grieg!"

Wanda swallowed.

"Er—yes. I estimate his height—without the hat —as being somewhere between six-foot-one and six-foot-two."

The FBI man's eyebrows went up.

"*So* exact? How can you be so sure, honey?"

"Because my brother Ed is the same height. Six-foot one and a half. I—my eyes came to the same level on the man as they do on Ed. When I look straight forward."

"And how tall would you say I am?"

Wanda looked at Mr. Willis with narrowed eyes. She moved closer and continued staring that way.

"A shade under six feet. Say five-eleven and a half. Uh—in your shoes, of course."

For the first time, the man smiled. He turned to Lieutenant Kaspar.

"Dead on target, Lieutenant!"

The lieutenant grunted. A little of the color was returning to his face. He gave Wanda a nod, then turned to McGurk.

"What else?"

"Joey here has something on his voice," said McGurk. "Officer Rockaway keeps our records. He's good at words. Officer Rockaway!"

"Sir," I said, "I am pretty sure the man is a Canadian. Or comes from one of the border states where they speak like Canadians."

The FBI man's eyes narrowed.

"What makes you say that?"

"His *ow* sounds, sir. Like in *about*. It sounded more like *aboot* or *abewt*."

"You sure?"

"Positive, sir."

"Great!" said the agent. "You getting all this down, Lieutenant?"

Lieutenant Kaspar nodded, without looking up from the notes he was scribbling.

"Now Brains here," said McGurk, "he's our crime-lab expert. For faces and heights and things—his observation powers are—uh—kind of normal. But scientific *instruments*—any instruments really—"

"His watch," said Brains, unable to contain himself. "I got a good look at it. It was a Rolex Oyster perpetual day-date model. In stainless steel. With matching expandable bracelet."

This produced another lift of the eyebrows.

"You sure?" said the FBI man. "In such detail?" He put his hands behind his back. "What am *I* wearing, then?"

Brains blinked.

"I am not standing near enough to be sure of the exact make, sir. But it has a black face with luminous Roman numerals and a gold case. The band is natural pigskin."

The man nodded.

"Pretty good," he said.

But Brains hadn't finished.

"Now the lieutenant's watch, I've seen it several times. It's—uh—quite a cheap make really, but very reliable—self-winding, waterproof, and with—"

"All right, all right!" growled Kaspar, putting his left hand below the desk. "It happens to have sentimental value—and—uh—you're right—it *is* reliable —and that's what counts."

"Yes!" said McGurk, frowning at Brains. "Cheapness doesn't come into this, Officer Bellingham!"

"What about you, McGurk?" said the lieutenant. "What's *your* detail?"

McGurk drew himself up, smirked, patted his necktie.

"The nose," he said.

"Yeah!" said Willie. "I—"

"Not *your* nose, Officer Sandowsky! I'm saving that until the last. I mean the *man's* nose." He turned to the FBI agent. "You know how some people have clefts in their chins—like dimples? . . . Well, this guy had one on his nose. At the end. It could have been an old scar. But anyway—a cleft."

The FBI man gasped. I can't swear to it that he said "Wow!"—but it sounded pretty close.

"Lieutenant," he said, "you really *did* mean what you said, didn't you? These kids really are—"

"Sure! Sure!"

Lieutenant Kaspar's eyes had a proud, pleased glow—but he shot the FBI man a warning look. I guess he's getting to know McGurk as well as the rest of us by now. Especially how quickly praise can go to our leader's head.

"Anything else?" he asked crisply.

Again McGurk drew himself up.

"Yes, sir!"

And this was where he proved it yet again: *smug and obnoxious as he can get about his own triumphs, he's always willing to give us credit where it is due.*

Like he'd said, he'd been saving the best—Willie's contribution—for the end. Willie's and Brains's, that is.

He even allowed Brains to introduce it.

"Well, sir," our science expert began, "Willie here has a remarkably sensitive nose. He can pick up scents most other noses miss completely. Like for instance the gum smell that indicated the man was wearing a phony beard."

"Hm!" The FBI man looked a bit disappointed. "Is that it, then?"

"No, sir. There was another, stronger smell, which Willie was able to identify—"

"Yeah. Aftershave!"

The FBI man shook his head slowly.

"Well—O.K. But so many men *do* use aftershave."

"Not this kind!" said Willie, firmly. "This was very unusual."

"Yes, but how—?"

"I know what you're thinking, sir," said Brains. "A sensitive nose is fine for tracking and tracing things and people. But how can it be used for accurate identification purposes? *Scientifically?* Right?"

The man nodded.

"Well," said Brains, "I'd been thinking about this,

too. And I decided there ought to be a system of ratings. So you can make accurate *smellprints*."

"*Smellprints?!*"

"Yes. The way we have fingerprints and—voice-prints."

The men looked at each other. McGurk beamed at Brains.

"The *smellsheets*, Officer Bellingham. Show them the *smellsheets*."

Brains nodded and took from his pocket the little stapled pad of graph paper that he'd run home to get earlier.

"This is a blank," he said, tearing one off and placing it on the desk.

The men stared at it.

Here is a copy:

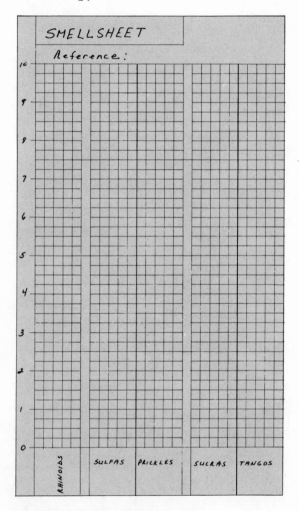

"Rhinoids?" said the lieutenant.

"It's a word I invented myself," said Brains. "It comes from a Greek word meaning nose. Like in rhinoceros. On the smellsheet it gives the *strength* of a smell, its *power*—on a scale of one to ten."

"Yeah—and that aftershave rates eight!" said Willie.

"So," said Brains, taking out a felt-tip pen, "we mark that rating on the sheet. Eight rhinoids."

He drew a heavy zigzag line down the rhinoids column, from eight to zero.

"Now we come to the tricky bit," said Brains. "Most smells you can divide into two kinds. I mean aside from their strength."

"Like whether they're a heavy, dirty, bad-eggsy kind of smell—" Willie began.

"Which I've marked in *sulfas*, since sulfur is the chemical base of that sort," explained Brains.

"Or sweet smells," said Willie.

"Which I've rated here in *sucras*—from the French word for sugar."

"I *see*. . . ." murmured the FBI man. "And *prickles* —I suppose that measures the pungency of a sulfa-type smell?"

"Yeah—the prickliness," said Willie.

"And *tangos*?" said the lieutenant.

"Its *tanginess*," said Willie. "Like the *zing*—uh— the *sharpness*—of a sweet smell."

"Its *tang*," I said, simply.

"So in this case—?" said the FBI man.

"The sulfa quality was very low," said Brains. "Right, Willie?"

Willie frowned, wrinkled his nose, screwed up his eyes—then nodded.

"Yeah. I guess. Just give it two or three of those little squares above the zero mark."

Brains did this.

"The prickles you can go a bit higher with," said Willie. He closed his eyes again. "Yeah. Give it just over a *one*."

Brains gave it just over a *one*.

"But basically it was a sweet smell," said Brains. "Right, Willie?"

"You bet!" said Willie. "Not rating as high as some women's perfumes. But way up, for an after-shave. Make it seven. Yeah. Just a shade over seven."

"And the sharpness?"

"Very. A real nose-cutter," said Willie. "For a nose like mine, I mean."

"So—how many tangos?"

"Nearly the tops. Give it a nine."

Brains made this final mark.

We were now left with a complete smellprint of the man's aftershave.

Here it is:

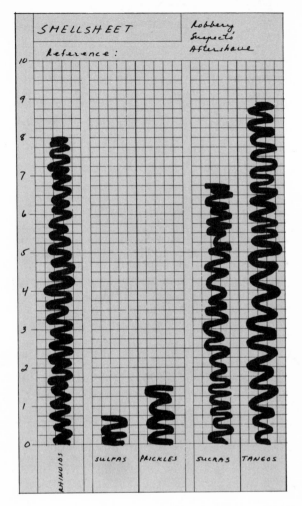

The agent and lieutenant looked at each other.

"You know what I'm thinking, Leonard?"

"I think so, Hedley."

"I'm thinking that if this guy has any kind of record at all, we'll be able to track him down in no time."

The FBI man turned to us.

"Kids," he said, "I can't tell you how helpful all this might be. Of course, the man may not have a record—in which case we'd be plain unlucky. But I'm going to wire all these details through to Central Records right away."

"Including the smellsheet?" said Brains.

"Well, yes—a summary of its indications. Now, if we are lucky, it'll take no more than a few hours. Maybe overnight. But I promise you I'll let you know the results as soon as I have them. I might even need to ask a few follow-up questions. Where can I reach you?"

McGurk told him. The lieutenant got up and led us to the door. The FBI man was already on the phone.

"You did well," murmured the lieutenant, looking much better now. He paused and looked thoughtfully at Willie. "Uh—how would *my* aftershave rate on the smellsheet?"

Willie wrinkled his nose again and started squeezing his eyes.

"Never mind!" said Lieutenant Kaspar, hurriedly. "Forget it. . . ."

Then he closed the door on us—no doubt anxious to get on with the job of putting our information to the best possible use.

12 The Final Detail

Special Agent Willis came around to our HQ late the following morning. McGurk had made three phone calls to Lieutenant Kaspar's office earlier, begging for the latest information, only to be told to sit tight and wait for the FBI man, who was still busy following up on the leads we'd given him. Other than that, the police would say nothing.

No wonder we all clustered around Mr. Willis as soon as he'd stepped inside.

"Any luck?"

"Did you get him?"

"Was there a shoot-out?"

"Is he outside in the car, waiting for us to identify him?"

Mr. Willis was smiling as he shook his head. But it wasn't the white-toothed smile we'd seen yesterday. His lips were pretty tight. I began to get a sinking feeling.

"We have a man in custody, yes," he said, glancing around at the newly tidied basement: at the rows of files set neatly on the table; the copying machine; my typewriter; the cameras; the big magnifying glass; and the handcuffs gleaming on their nail in the wall behind McGurk's chair.

"Here, sir—sit here," said McGurk, offering him that chair.

"Thank you," said the agent.

"So you got him then?" said McGurk, squeezing his hands together and hovering like he was a butler or something.

"Well," said the agent, "I said we had him in custody. Whether we can *keep* him there. . . ." He broke off with a sigh.

"Did he fit the details we gave you?" asked Wanda.

"The details fit *him*, yes," said our visitor. "Which isn't quite the same thing."

Some of us were beginning to look puzzled. Only Willie didn't seem to sense there was something wrong.

"*All* the details?" he asked eagerly. "Including—"

"The aftershave? Yes, Willie." The man gave another weary smile. "Seems he got hooked on a special brand he picked up in Mexico a few years back. Uh—*Viva Zapata*, it's called."

"And the watch?" asked Brains.

"Just as you said. *And* his height. *And* the fact that he was born and brought up in Toronto. *And* the cleft in his nose."

"Well, then," said McGurk, beginning to beam again, "we've got him cold!"

The man was frowning. He seemed deep in thought. McGurk's grin faded.

"He *did* have a record?" I said. "I mean for you to be able to trace him so fast?"

"Oh, sure!" said the man. "Even a prior arrest and conviction on a bank robbery charge ten years ago. But—as I was trying to say earlier—all these details do is to point strongly to the fact that he was *here*, in this room. And of course that he was involved in the bank job."

He paused.

"But—?" said Wanda.

"But it doesn't add up to absolute proof. Especially since it wasn't even at the scene of the crime that you saw him. Not even the same day. With the alibi he claims to have, a good lawyer would probably get him acquitted."

"Alibi?" said McGurk. "What alibi?"

"On both days, he claims he was in Philadelphia, visiting with his brother-in-law. And since his brother-in-law has no previous record—even though we've had strong suspicions about him for a long time—well. . . ." The agent shrugged. "That would strengthen his case."

McGurk looked ready to burst into tears of baffled indignation.

"So you're going to let him *go?*"

Again the man shrugged.

"Unless we find something that proves conclusively he was here, in this town—or shake his alibi in some other way—yes. We can't hold him much longer, merely on suspicion. *However* strong that suspicion is," he added quickly, when McGurk looked like firing off another outburst.

"Like *what*, sir?" asked Brains. "*What* would prove conclusively he was here?"

"Like fingerprints. A fingerprint, even. In this room. At the bank." The agent sighed. "But of course that would be the first thing he'd guard against." He looked around at us glumly. "You say he was muffled up against the cold? I suppose that included gloves?"

We looked at one another. Then nodded.

"The only time I can remember him taking them off was when he was pretending to make notes," I said.

"And when he showed us the phony card," said McGurk. "But of course he took *that* back."

"Yes," I said. "I wondered at the time why he didn't leave it with us."

"He also removed his gloves when he looked at the picture," said Brains. "Or maybe they were already off. Anyhow, that's how I got a good look at his watch."

The FBI man nodded.

"It figures. The only things a guy like that would touch with his bare hands would be the things he meant to take with him." He looked around again. "You say he pretended to take an interest in this —uh—equipment?"

"Yes, sir," I said. "But it was pretty half-baked. I mean he bent to look at the stuff—"

"Yeah! Like the copying machine," said Willie. "That's when I smelled his—"

"But he never *touched* any of it," I said, sticking to the point.

"Not even the handcuffs when I held them out to him," said McGurk, sadly. He groaned. *"To think we could have snapped them on his wrists!"*

"Oh, well—never mind," said Mr. Willis, standing up. "Maybe something will turn up at the bank." He smiled. "But don't let it get you down. It wasn't your fault."

He bent to the table, taking a closer look at the files.

"And I must say you seem to run a very tight ship here, McGurk."

"Sir?"

"Very efficient. Very thorough."

McGurk brightened. After all, this *was* praise. And praise from a real FBI agent at that!

"Yes, sir!"

"The records are *my* responsibility," I said, seeing the man's interest in the box marked LATEST MYSTERY—RECORDS & CLUES.

"Very neat," said Mr. Willis. He reached out to the two big envelopes already in there. With big black letters, I'd labeled one: #1 CAMERA PATROL (BANKS)—WEDNESDAY P.M.—and the other: #2 CAMERA PATROL (BANKS)—THURSDAY A.M. "May I?"

"Go ahead!" said McGurk. "Those are the pictures we took in the streets. Like for if there'd been a holdup around the same time," he added, his face clouding again as he thought of our missed opportunity on Friday.

I think Mr. Willis was only trying to be kind, showing an interest like this. As he spread the Wednesday pictures on the table, he made no comment about the bad ones taken by McGurk.

But when he came to look at the Thursday pictures his whole attitude changed.

"Hmm." he murmured, picking one up and peering at it closely. "You say you took these on Thursday?"

"Yes, sir," said Brains. "That's another of McGurk's flops, though. He'd improved a lot, but not with that one."

We knew what Brains meant. Here is that picture:

"Well the woman got in the *way!*" said McGurk. "And anyway, we were just about to go into the bank. I wasn't really concentrating. It was just another guy with a long loose coat."

"*Him* I'm not interested in," murmured the agent, still peering. "The guy with the short plaid car-coat across the street there *does* interest me. Pass me that magnifying glass, son."

I handed him the glass. He peered again.

And then we *did* see the wide white smile.

"Well, well, well!" he murmured. "What do you know? If it isn't the brother-in-law himself! The guy who says the suspect was with him in Philadelphia all day Thursday and right up to five P.M. yesterday!"

We clustered around.

"You sure, sir?"

"Positive. And when we get this blown up, no lawyer on earth is going to help them wriggle out of it." He turned. "Now you *can* swear on oath that this was taken on Thursday morning, right outside the bank?"

"Absolutely!" said McGurk.

"Between 9:30 and 10 A.M.," said Brains. "I can swear to that, too."

"Exactly when the suspect was casing the inside of the bank," said Wanda. "This one must have been casing the *outside!*"

The FBI man grinned as he carefully slipped the snapshot into his wallet.

"The very thing we needed," he said. "I think we can safely say your Organization has chalked up another triumph, McGurk!"

He was right. By breaking the phony reporter's alibi, our picture enabled the police and FBI to arrest the brother-in-law and charge him as an accessory to the robbery. And since the brother-in-law wasn't as hard-nosed as his relative, he soon broke down and confessed everything. He was even able to identify the woman "hostage" and say exactly where the money had been stashed.

Naturally, all this took several days to tidy up and was strictly a matter for the police, the FBI and the attorneys. As far as *we* were concerned, the case was closed that morning—and closed successfully.

Which in a way was a bad thing for some of us. Why?

Because it meant that McGurk was highly satis-

fied. And when McGurk is highly satisfied with one thing, he immediately turns his attention to something else.

On this occasion, the "something else" was just what I'd already feared.

The FBI man hadn't been gone more than ten minutes before McGurk clapped his hands.

"Hey! All this has made me forget."

"Forget what, McGurk?"

"That it's almost New Year's!"

"So?"

"So we should be working out our New Year's resolutions. As an Organization."

I sighed.

"Oh, yes?"

"Yeah! And now that we're kind of—uh—*associate* FBI agents ourselves, I think we should start by tightening up on the Organization dress code!"

Didn't I tell you?

I only hope we'll never get involved in a case with the Canadian Mounties, because—believe me —Jack P. McGurk would have us wearing red coats and blue riding breeches before we could say "Saskatchewan!"